D0823383

2 A.M.
IN LITTLE
AMERICA

ALSO BY KEN KALFUS

Coup de Foudre: A Novella and Stories
Equilateral: A Novel
A Disorder Peculiar to the Country: A Novel
The Commissariat of Enlightenment: A Novel
Pu-239 and Other Russian Fantasies:
A Novella and Stories
Thirst: Stories

2 A.M.
IN LITTLE
AMERICA

a novel

KEN KALFUS

MILKWEED EDITIONS

8/26/22.
For Kevin,
All best wishes
a *th* thanks!
— Ken

The characters and events in this book are fictitious. Any similarity to real persons, living or dead, is coincidental and not intended by the author.

© 2022, Text by Ken Kalfus

All rights reserved. Except for brief quotations in critical articles or reviews, no part of this book may be reproduced in any manner without prior written permission from the publisher: Milkweed Editions, 1011 Washington Avenue South, Suite 300, Minneapolis, Minnesota 55415.

(800) 520-6455

milkweed.org

First paperback edition, published in 2022 by Milkweed Editions
Printed in the United States of America
Cover design and illustration by Mary Austin Speaker
Cover photograph by Kramer O'Neill
22 23 24 25 26   5 4 3 2 1
First Edition

978-1-63955-077-7

Part of this novel appeared on the *n + 1* website, nplusonemag.com.

Library of Congress Cataloging-in-Publication Data

Names: Kalfus, Ken, author.
Title: 2 a.m. in Little America : a novel / Ken Kalfus.
Description: First edition. | Minneapolis, Minnesota : Milkweed Editions, 2022.
Identifiers: LCCN 2021044847 (print) | LCCN 2021044848 (ebook) | ISBN 9781571311443 (hardcover ; acid-free paper) | ISBN 9781571317735 (ebook)
Subjects: LCGFT: Novels. Classification: LCC PS3561.A416524 A613 2022 (print) | LCC PS3561.A416524 (ebook) | DDC 813/.54--dc23
LC record available at https://lccn.loc.gov/2021044847
LC ebook record available at https://lccn.loc.gov/2021044848

Milkweed Editions is committed to ecological stewardship. We strive to align our book production practices with this principle, and to reduce the impact of our operations in the environment. We are a member of the Green Press Initiative, a nonprofit coalition of publishers, manufacturers, and authors working to protect the world's endangered forests and conserve natural resources. *2 A.M. in Little America* was printed on acid-free 30% postconsumer-waste paper by Versa Press.

For Inga and Sky

2 A.M.
IN LITTLE
AMERICA

I

Like many people my age, I found myself in a foreign city where I took a low-paying job in a semi-menial field that I hadn't previously contemplated. This work wasn't unpleasant. It brought me several times a day up to the city's rooftops, above the traffic noises, where I was surrounded by the pinnacles of the city's most ambitious skyscrapers and I caught views of its churning bay and the forested mountains in the distance. I would usually need about a half hour to check the security equipment that I was assigned to certify as operational. I would repair it if necessary. Then in good weather I would take a few minutes to savor the prospect and the occasional sea breezes so that I could recall them later, as I went to bed. I worked alone, with my own thoughts. I hoped to keep the job indefinitely, or at least until my visa situation became untenable.

The equipment was often put in awkward locations on the roofs, sometimes in crawl spaces or on walls that could be reached only with my portable step stool. On the warm afternoon when I first saw the woman who would come to occupy a sizable but uncertain place in my imagination, I had been sent to a medium-rise building on the city's less affluent north side. The apartment house was several decades old and, like many other buildings, it had been augmented by extra stories and ad hoc structures to accommodate the recent influx of city residents, mostly foreign migrants and people from the country's rural areas. After taking the elevator to the sixth floor, I climbed another flight to reach the door to the upper roof. The unit's control panel was mounted waist-high to a brick wall squeezed between two rooftop additions.

I recalled that I had inspected the same unit once before. It had worked normally then. Squatting on the balls of my feet, mostly in shadow, I now opened the panel. Several tests confirmed that the circuit board needed replacement. I disconnected the power and jimmied out the board. There was a new one in my toolbox. I worked on the installation with my usual absorption, even though I was aware that someone had turned on a light in one of the new flats behind me and was moving around. Water was running. I retested the unit and put back my tools.

I rose, turned to go, and took a step past the screened open window between the flat's cinder block lower wall and its aluminum-sided upper section. The window was apparently located in the flat's bathroom, where a woman was taking a shower, her back to the showerhead, the front of her body facing the window. I recoiled as if I had seen something horrible, which I hadn't. I pushed myself back against the wall where the control panel was located. I didn't want to surprise her or do anything furtive that could provoke a call to the police. I waited a minute, thinking about my next step. The water stopped. I had barely seen her, no more than a flash of alarmingly naked wet skin.

I had worked for some time in this job, roaming across the city's roofs. Nothing like this had ever happened before. I hoped the woman would draw her shade, but the long, low window may have provided the flat's only ventilation. Many of this teeming neighborhood's first rooftop additions had been broken into even smaller flats, leaving some with strangely sized rooms, improvisational kitchens and bathrooms, and inconveniently placed windows. Warm, moist air streamed from the window screen, rippling the deep-blue late afternoon sky above my head. I smelled soap possibly scented with something citrus.

My presence on the roof was easily explained, of course, and my story would be confirmed by my employer. If the police were called, however, they would be obliged to inspect my visa and my work papers. The documents were mostly in order, but not entirely: one stamp was missing and another had expired, and perhaps there were other problems of which I wasn't aware. The residency rules were always changing. Yet I couldn't hide against the wall indefinitely; that on its own would raise suspicions, if I were seen from one of the neighboring buildings.

The only thing to do was to announce myself. I ran a hand through my hair and straightened the creases in my uniform shirt. Squaring my shoulders, I stepped directly in front of the window screen. Half averting my eyes, I put on a face that expressed abject regret and embarrassment, and I lifted the toolbox to show the woman why I was there. I was about to mumble a few words of apology that would have been fully sincere.

She stood before me and held a flower-patterned towel away from her side. She was air-drying for now while she tried to pull a troublesome tangle from her just-washed hair. She hadn't flinched when I suddenly appeared, even though she was looking in my direction. Her eyes were open wide. Her lips were pursed in thought. She evidently didn't see me. A spell cast by the room's internal lighting, the dimness in the space between the rooftop structures, and the dense screen, meant to keep out the city's endemic gnat swarms, had rendered me invisible. She herself was perfectly seen, from her crown of wet hair to her feet. The image washed over me like a wave. I realized then that the woman was an image in fact: she wasn't at the window as I first thought, but standing in front of a slightly fogged full-length mirror attached to the inside of the open bathroom door, opposite the window. Yet I remained in her line of sight. I raised my toolbox again and mouthed another apology at the reflection. She still didn't see me.

Now that I was in the clear, I should have left the roof and continued on my way, but after another moment at the window I fell back against the wall that held the repaired control panel, the woman's nakedness still filling my eyes.

The threat of being caught was real; any legal offense risked my deportation. The chance I took by remaining on the roof ran counter to every instinct for self-preservation that had governed my life since I went abroad. There had been several close calls, but not from any recklessness on my part.

I had also avoided doing wrong, or at least I had avoided doing anything wrong that was not necessary for my survival. I was aware now that in having watched her through the window screen I had gratuitously trespassed on the woman's right to privacy—a principle that may have fallen into desuetude in the current century, yet a value or quality that I scrounged for in my own exacting days and disturbed nights. And the ridiculous words "Peeping Tom" still carried opprobrium, signifying a pathetic transgression that reminded the Tom of his sexual want.

This reminded me of my sexual want. I had not been with a woman in years. In these years, in my twenties, I had suffered many privations, not being with a woman laughably the least of them, but I was keenly conscious that it had been a long time, on another continent, since I observed a woman's smile of tender affection, or been the target of a flirtatious sally, or been anyone's romantic possibility, or been offered the most fleeting view of a woman's bare, rude, robust animal body. I was ashamed by my impulse; at the same time I knew that if I returned to the window screen, and if the woman didn't see me, I wouldn't be taking anything from her or doing anything that would bring her harm or in any way intrude upon her existence. To turn away now, and to not be present for her ordinary female beauty, would have been an offense against myself, I thought, a denial of my humanness, a denial of life.

I stepped before the window and again made a sign of apology. It was not met with a response. The woman, who was about my age, still fussed with her hair. The mirror's reflection gave her the appearance of being no more than four feet away. The day was humid and drops from the shower still glistened on her limbs. As she leaned over to reach her lower legs, they tensed. She continued to gaze at herself in the mirror, right at me. I took this in hungrily, just as I had taken in my views of the city's skyline, its bay, and the countryside, with the intention and conviction that I would never forget them.

Her face was pretty, though perhaps not conventionally so, or perhaps it was conventionally pretty but transformed by the liberties taken by my covert observation. I looked into the depths of her eyes. They suggested, to me in this moment, receptiveness and sympathy. I gifted myself the thought of what it might be like to be kissed by this woman. As I stared, I wondered if I had seen the woman before. Of course, I *had* seen her before, only two minutes earlier, when I passed in front of the window screen as she came out of the shower, and then again a few moments later when I looked back, and again in the past thirty or forty seconds, when I was directing at her the entirety of my attention. I was aware that this was likely an illusion of familiarity, with which I had some previous experience, discovering that it could arise in any close quarters, say in a café or on a train. You notice somebody, they make a strong impression, and then when you see them again shortly later, the first instance feels like a long-standing memory. Disembarking from a long international flight, I often felt that I had known some of the passengers my whole life, though I was acquainted with them only from having observed them walking to and from the toilets or reaching for their blankets in the overhead bins. The sense that I might recognize this woman was the same kind of self-deception, I told myself. But I found the thought unpersuasive. I continued to wonder if she was someone I had once seen in the street, or on the Corniche, or on a bus. Or was she someone I had known in the past, from my first travels, or from even before then? Could she possibly be an American?

Some vague recollection stirred, but I didn't trust it. I knew how intensely I thought of America, how regularly I imagined myself there, walking the shady, cracked, root-heaved sidewalks of the small community in which I had grown up, or entering the diner, or taking my position on the county ball field. At night whatever dreams made sense usually took place in America; when I woke I was often surprised to find myself abroad. It might take me several moments to remember where or especially why, a complicated series of causes and effects. In my daily life on the streets of this foreign city I couldn't stop looking for things and people that were at least remotely connected to America, evidence that the place still existed. I wondered now if this intense longing for home had somehow conjured my sense of half familiarity with the woman, the object of a parallel, not-too-dissimilar kind of longing.

The woman's hair had been untangled and she made some private smile at a private thought, though of course the smile was not as private as she believed. I wished I could know the thought that inspired it. Then she turned and reached somewhere beyond the edge of the mirror's image. The bare expanse of her back was presented like a pristine, unpopulated territory. When she faced the mirror again she held a pair of black plastic-rimmed eyeglasses in her hands and I realized that a component of my invisibility might have been her near-sightedness. She raised the glasses to her face. Without

even a lingering last look, careful not to kick the gravel
on the surface of the roof, I moved quickly from the window. Two more assignments were left to my day.

✦

I didn't tell anyone about this odd, happy adventure. I
suppose if I had some close male friends, as I once had
in another life, I might have related the story excitedly:
You wouldn't believe what just happened to me! I would
have elaborated upon my rooftop predicament. My bud-
dies would have been amused. Perhaps raising a toast to
her beauty, they might have even shared similarly provi-
dential experiences. Now, among my few acquaintances,
some from countries with unpredictable, stringent
mores regarding the male gaze and the female body, the
story would have been embarrassing and a confession of
wrongdoing, even untrustworthiness.

I wouldn't have told any of the men with whom I
shared a flat, which was located in a cinder block mid-
rise near the beltway, on a desiccated plain of cinder
block mid-rises. We kept a wary distance from each other
and from each other's personal illegalities. There were
nine of us, three to a cell-like room, all of us migrants, all
still learning the local language, all with probable visa
infractions.

None were Americans and I knew very few com-
patriots abroad. Americans kept away from each other

then. We were humiliated by what had happened; we would have reminded each other only of our grief and our shame. Also, when two Americans met, you couldn't know which side the other had joined, nor what actions that person had taken, nor what he or she had suffered. In going abroad we had shed the many indicators of partisanship—haircuts, clothing choices—to fit in more easily among the local people, if that was possible, or at least to gain some anonymity among the population of migrants from other countries. We tried to remain invisible to each other.

I certainly didn't advertise my nationality among non-Americans. People around the world shared contempt for how far our country had fallen. Some of that contempt was expressed with pleasure. They recalled our former national pride, which they had considered, even at the time, vain and overweening. They remembered too how we had dominated international politics and global popular culture and the many errors, or crimes, we had committed at home and abroad, now under investigation by an international commission. They remembered the sanctimony. They remembered the lectures. They remembered the displays of entitlement. The wars too. They were glad for our comeuppance even when it had presented difficulties for their own countries. Some of these countries had inevitably replayed American political arguments and social disputes, adapted to their histories. They were bitter about that as well. My paperwork showed that I was a United States citizen, but in casual conversation I might say that I was Canadian, and I occasionally found myself pretending familiarity with the city of Toronto.

Not speaking of the woman didn't mean I forgot her, of course. I remembered everything I had seen. She was added to a small, vital archive. When I was alone, or trying to be alone, I deliberately flipped through the files. Unable to sleep, buffeted by the snores and other night sounds of my flatmates, or crammed into a bus to or from the city's untidy outskirts, I would summon certain images to mind. I could, for example, almost re-create my hometown and see myself driving my parents' car to the stores, passing every mailbox and gas station, block by block. Or I thought of this city's skyline and the vistas of the bay that I had more recently observed, capturing pleasing details that I might have missed at first. Or, as I did many times in the next few days, almost in a trance, I illuminated on the screen of my consciousness a picture of the woman's hale unclothed self: every curve, every hair, the hollows of her ankles, her contemplative expression. These memories, significant to me alone, belonging to me alone, represented a kind of sanctuary.

Although my thoughts dwelled on the woman, I never seriously considered returning to the roof of the building to spy on her. It would have been dangerous to be seen lurking there and I knew anyway that I couldn't replicate the conditions of sun and shadow that had made me unseeable. Also, it would have been simply too pervy. What I had already done had at least bumped up against the edge of wrongness. But I felt free to think of her nakedness without restraint and I hoped I would see her again somewhere. I thought we might somehow meet. I thought we might find a way to exchange a few words. I intently looked into the faces of the women around me on the city's packed sidewalks and public transportation.

I was hardly surprised, then, a couple of weeks later when I encountered her crossing the square in front of the city's main cathedral, for it felt as if my relentless visualizing had beamed the woman directly into this place. I saw her from forty or fifty meters, coming at me, navigating the cobblestones in modestly heeled shoes. She wore what I supposed was an office outfit, a snug midlength gray skirt, a white button-down blouse, and a short red jacket, open in the seasonable weather. Her now-dry hair was shaped in what was then a fashionable style. It was near lunchtime and she was carrying an unopened yogurt container and a plastic spoon. We were only a few blocks from her flat.

As she approached I looked her in the face long enough to appreciate her features and to make an effort to remember how they presented themselves at the moment. I took note of her mouth, now sharply lipsticked, her eyes, and the shape of her eyebrows. She wasn't wearing the glasses; perhaps she wore contact lenses whenever she left the flat. The woman didn't detect my interest any more than she had when I was on the roof. I avoided eye contact and then turned away so that my scrutiny wouldn't be obvious. She was really quite lovely, I thought.

We went by each other and I continued on for several meters. Then slowly, so as not to attract attention from the other passersby, I turned to watch her go. She dodged a puddle left from the recent rains. Other pedestrians swirled around me. After a few moments there was a small letup in her gait and she also seemed about to stop and turn, as if she sensed my eyes on her. I didn't really think this awareness was possible, though people often spoke of it and I may have read that the phenomenon had been observed in animals.

Regardless of my skepticism, I went on my way, my ears burning from the embarrassment of nearly being caught—at what, looking at a pretty woman on the square? I suppose I blushed instead from fear that I would still be found out for my first misconduct. But by the time I boarded the tram that took me to my next service call, I began to doubt that the woman was the same person I had seen in the flat. The determined frame of this woman's face was different from the more open, vulnerable expression on the other's, and the features may not have been precisely identical—one, with more widely spaced eyes, the other with a sharper nose? I couldn't be sure that this woman's hair was cut similarly to the hair I had seen wet from the shower. And now the face of the woman in the square was fresher in my mind, blurring the image of the original.

I inwardly smiled at my confusion. This was a petty vexation compared to the other difficulties in my life—there was some question about how much longer I could keep my bed in the flat; a hole had declared itself on the bottom of my irreplaceable right shoe—but I knew too that the brief moment on the roof was still something I would hold dear.

After this nonmeeting on the plaza, I saw the woman again, once in the window of a café in her neighborhood, sipping an espresso, and then in another part of town, where she was leaving an office building with some colleagues or friends, and again I couldn't make a positive identification with the woman in the flat. I couldn't even be sure that these additional sightings were of the same person, especially after I saw her again in another neighborhood, wearing a worker's denim overalls, and again elsewhere, in yet other neighborhoods, with longer hair and wire-rimmed eyeglasses and stouter, shorter, or more pale than I remembered her, or apparently affiliated with another ethnicity, or pushing a baby carriage. I realized now that all the women of the city were gradually coming to resemble in my mind the woman who had been in the flat that afternoon, and this was a good thing, for now I made my rounds, crowded into one conveyance or another, in a slightly elevated state of desire, something I had hardly felt since I left the States. I enjoyed traveling among these women. They were imbued with life, optimism, and high-spirited sexuality, it seemed. I listened attentively to their songlike conversations. I deeply inhaled their sweet, complicated scents, every one her own. Through these women—even though I thought they were beyond the possible acquaintance of a penniless migrant—I developed a stronger connection to the city and I began to think of it as something like home.

✦

It's not unusual for migrants to voice this sentiment prematurely. A few months later, but not so much later that I had forgotten the woman, the country in which I was living experienced a period of political turmoil. New immigration laws were passed in response. These were strict laws, it seemed, but they still had to work their way through the courts, some of the provisions were complicated, and I was unsure how they would affect my status. Anti-immigration activists, inside and outside the legislature, didn't think the laws went far enough. This view was expressed with small-scale violence: broken shop windows and assaults of people who looked like they could be migrants. The pro-immigration forces, such as they were, suggested that the governing party was provoking its militant opponents in order to make itself seem more moderate. Further appeasing the angry nativists, the government withdrew its support of the international investigative commission before it could interview witnesses.

Around this time the flat was taken over by a gang that had moved into the area. I arrived one evening and found my few things picked through and dumped in the hallway. I couldn't protest. I spent that night and the next at the company where I worked, sleeping in the unheated equipment shed through the indulgence of a semi-friendly, semi-negligent watchman. I then obtained, through a series of faint connections, a place in another tenement, or rather a still-warm, still-fragrant nighttime bed occupied during the day by a migrant with a nocturnal work schedule. I had to be out by five a.m.

I continued to conduct my inspections and repairs. A few days after I began sleeping in the new place, I was given an assignment to check equipment located on the roof of a large department store. I headed on foot along the city's main commercial boulevard, carrying my toolbox. Gloomily absorbed with the problems that were presented by my new living arrangements, I may have put aside my customary alertness and didn't recognize that trouble was collecting itself up ahead.

Other pedestrians were more aware. They turned and streamed back down the sidewalk, not on a panicked run, but determined to get away. I went another half block before I stopped.

The disturbance was either a march or a demonstration, which were generally legal, but it appeared to be

unauthorized and the government hadn't given the protesters a place to rally. Mostly men, most of them young,
they moved down the sidewalk in our direction. They
waved football flags and chanted anti-immigrant slogans.
Some of the flags were attached to sticks. The police, lined
along the curb in the street, had evidently been ordered
to keep the roadway unblocked. The boulevard was a
vital traffic corridor whose easy flow was valued by the
city government as a measure of its competence. Also, the
national government was showing its resolve against the
opposition. The shops had locked up and lowered their
grilles. Pedestrians could only go back, where, when I
turned, I saw a squad of helmeted riot police massing in
the plaza in front of the government offices. But the government hadn't anticipated a march of this size.

The police arrayed along the side of the road were
aware of this miscalculation. They didn't have visors
or other equipment with which to face a hostile crowd.
A sergeant frantically consulted with a superior over a
walkie-talkie, trying to explain how the sidewalk was
becoming congested. If the march was going to be kept
on the sidewalk, they needed to allow the pedestrians into
the street. We heard the order in return, squawked from
the radio: keep traffic moving. The other cops looked
harassed and worried. They were young, possibly new
recruits. There were nowhere near enough of them.

I expected to be punched or spat upon—this had
happened before—but hoped that I would then be

allowed to go on my way. The people around me didn't share my feeble optimism. As the knot tightened, some became anxious about the potential for serious violence and others increasingly indignant. Several women, probably native-born, abused the cops for their haplessness. A few pedestrians tried to step off the curb but the police gripped both ends of their nightsticks and pushed them back onto the sidewalk, forcefully but not without sympathy. They called for reinforcements in vain. Cars and trucks continued to pass at nearly normal speeds.

I allowed myself to be buffeted by the surging crowd. I looked down at my feet as the marchers approached, trying to make myself even more anonymous than usual. I fiercely held on to the toolbox. My first priority was not to lose it in a scuffle or a chase.

The sergeant finally took charge of the problem, improvisationally. Waving his black-and-white striped traffic stick, he pulled over a private van. The driver scowled, but he didn't protest when the police ordered it open and told the trapped pedestrians to get on board. The man drove off into the traffic with them. A second windowed van, emblazoned with the logo for the airport shuttle service, was brought to the curb next. It too was nearly empty. The door opened and one of the cops pushed me in. The march was almost upon us.

He packed the vehicle until it was completely jammed. I kept my toolbox on my lap as we pulled into the roadway. We needed only to pass the government offices, where the police were setting up barricades, but now traffic was unavoidably slowed by the belated arrival of three army trucks, which occupied two lanes. My cotravelers began ridiculing the cops for being so thickheaded, and then the politicians for creating the situation, and then the protesters, and then someone added that further demonstrations and riots were inevitable as long as there were so many migrants. Murmurs of concurrence washed over us. I kept to myself, gazing onto the opposite, uncongested side of the street, where I thought I saw the woman I had been looking for, and now I also thought that she could be either two or three of my fellow passengers.

These were foolish distractions. My main concern was getting to the roof of the department store. I would have to take the subway several stops, pass under the protest, and reach the store from the other side. I wondered near which metro station the driver would let us off; the more convenient station was known for the stylish curves of its prewar architecture, though I was never sure which war it had preceded.

I looked up to the front of the van and saw the driver's eyes in the rearview mirror. They darted as she maneuvered the vehicle through the lurching, squealing traffic. I abruptly shifted my position, leaning my head against the window, so that I could see her face in the combination convex-aspheric side-view mirror. I knew

at once that this was the same woman I had observed on
the roof earlier in the year.

The features of the other women I thought I recognized vanished in a haze. This was clearly not the individual I had passed in the square, nor the person I had
seen in the window of the café nor several tables away in
the public library reading room, her head bowed above
a large-format art book, nor at the reception desk of the
office building I had serviced the day before yesterday.
This woman was as tangible as the van I was riding
in, the police in the street, and the city's towers rising
around us. I sensed that I had returned to the roof and
could now observe her in the side-view mirror as well
as I had in her bathroom's fogged mirror. Not only did
I identify the woman from that day, I knew from where
in the distant past she had seemed familiar. I checked
her again, marveling at the concatenation of departures
and arrivals, distant events and personal exigencies, and
traps and escapes that had led us to occupy the same
vehicle in a remote foreign city. She finally stopped the
van a few blocks away from the protest and let everyone
out, receiving praise and maternal kisses from several of
the women. I waited so that I would be the last to leave.

I stepped through the open door but didn't close it. I
grinned at the woman in the van's driver seat.

"Thank you, Amanda!" I said. "It's me, Ron Patterson,
from Kennedy. Eleventh-grade physics!"

She scanned my face in a moment and shook her

head. She smiled pleasantly. "English no," she said. In the local language, she explained, "I'm sorry, but I didn't understand you. I don't speak English."

"No, I'm sorry, I thought you were American," I said hurriedly in the same language, which I spoke semi-competently. I was aware of the faux pas. Non-Americans hated to be mistaken for American. "I thought you were someone I knew from high school. Back in the States. A girl named Amanda."

"Is that a common American name?" she asked. "It's pretty."

Sheepishly, I said, "It's not even someone I knew well. You reminded me of her for a moment, but she never rescued me from an angry mob. You're a regular hero."

As I gazed at her now, I realized I had erred again. She looked nothing like Amanda Keller, a girl I had probably spoken with no more than once or twice. In any case I hadn't seen her since high school, a number of eventful years in the past. I looked hard again. The driver remained in her seat, the van's engine still running. She smiled with amusement at my earnest study. I no longer thought she was Amanda, but I told myself that she could possibly be the woman from the roof.

"Ha. I'll look for my medal in the mail."

"Right," I said. "Well, thanks again." I gave her one last look, this time to remember everything about her, before sliding the door shut.

She was the friendliest person I had met in months, despite the mistaken identification. Her smile stayed with me and I did something that I would have never expected. I rushed around the van to the driver's side before she could pull into traffic. Her window was open.

"Hey," I said.

"Hey," she said back, but I saw in her eyes that my abrupt approach had startled her.

"Hey," I repeated. "Um, look," I said. "Hey. I hope this is not too weird, but would you like to come with me for a walk sometime? On the Corniche? I'm off Sundays. I walk there whenever the weather's half-decent."

She recovered her poise. I realized that her acute surprise had briefly been fearful, about which I again felt sorry. I would wonder later exactly what about me had frightened her, beyond a migrant's typical dishevelment.

"You're very demanding," she said dryly. "First I rescue you, now you want a date?"

"Not a date," I hastened to say, taking on a much more serious tone than hers. I pointed to my toolbox and my grimy, threadbare overalls as an explanation for why it wouldn't be a date. I had no money for dates or clothes, nor bright life prospects. "Just a walk. The Corniche is my favorite place in the city. I like to go from one end to the other, all the way to the Navy Yard, and then back again. But I won't make you walk the whole way."

She didn't reply, but I could tell she wasn't refusing the invitation out of hand. She was thinking about it, in fact. I felt something lift in my chest. I told her she didn't have to agree at once. I would be there anyway, on the east end of the embankment by the umbrella shack, at ten that Sunday morning.

"Please come," I said. "But only if you want to."

✦

The protesters that day were dispersed without further incident, but their unexpected numbers emboldened the organizers to demand closed streets for another march. This in turn obliged the official opposition to announce a rally that would fill the cathedral square. The government was forced to allow the protests, while insisting that it was already preparing further measures to control immigration. No one spoke of this at work or in the flat where I was living. It was best to keep our heads down when it came to the day's news.

The next Sunday was especially fine and I went to the waterfront as I said I would, crossing at a traffic light the six-lane highway that arced around the city's long, very busy bay. Sandwiched between the road and the beach, the broad, concrete Corniche was the place where the high-strung, hardworking city came to collect its thoughts. Couples and families with small children strolled the boardwalk. Artists set up easels. Vendors sold cold drinks, local and exotic pastries, and sweets, and buskers provided entertainment. At one place a small, low-energy amusement park had been established. The water in the bay was too dirty for swimming, but the beach was sandy and it brought sunbathers. A few pleasure boats drifted in the bay and in the distance you could see oceangoing tankers and cargo ships. I took a seat on the retaining wall near the umbrella shack, actually a cinder block cube whose green paint was flecked and peeling. The sky was pale with a high, wispy cloud cover and a breeze tentatively stirred up some whitecaps.

I never expected the woman to show and I also never expected the degree of my disappointment when she didn't. Nine forty-five. Ten. Ten fifteen. Ten thirty. I lowered myself from the wall to look around and make sure I could be seen. A few swimsuited, flip-flopped customers waited at the shack; a teenage boy brought their umbrellas down to the beach. A man came around selling fresh-cut fruit from his cart. Ten forty-five. I still hoped, urgently, that the van driver would appear. At the same time I wondered how unreasonable this hope was. I had never been the kind of guy who casually introduced himself to women, either on the street, for example, or in a bar. I had already signaled that I didn't have the means to entertain her. I was at best a significantly scruffy American. I was foolish to have conceived any kind of expectation on the basis of her good-naturedness.

I realized that the depth of my ill humor was yet another sign of just how lonely I was and also, probably, how these years of exile and indigence had made me a little deranged. The life I was living in my twenties was nothing as I had imagined it would be: I occupied a permanent state of disbelief. I had never expected to be *this* person, with whatever personal characteristics now manifested themselves. Indeed, I sometimes imagined, when my guard was down, that another self lived elsewhere, living a normal life in a normal country, a normal United States of America at peace. *This* person had a girlfriend or a wife, maybe kids, close friends, a steady job, and ordinary dreams. My fixation on the woman I had observed on the roof was just another indicator of a dislodged screw. I found it so difficult to accept the conditions of my actual existence that I was no longer sure what was real and what was not, what was possible and what was not possible.

I understood why my mind lingered on home, but I didn't know why I even recalled Amanda Keller, a girl with whom I had barely been acquainted. She sat a few rows behind me in physics and rarely spoke up, even though Mr. Strauss was a lively, entertaining teacher who tried to engage the entire class with hands-on experiments in wave motion, optics, and electrical conduction. The lab equipment was very cool. But Amanda and I were never lab partners. She once passed me a worksheet. That might have been the extent of our relations. I could have more logically focused my memories on sweet, caring Vanessa Hickman, my high school girlfriend. We had hung out all of junior year. We mostly listened to music together, with the other people in our circle, Dan and Monika, Ravi and Sarah, Audrey and Roberto. We held hands in the hallway. We made out in the stairwell. We made love in her bedroom when her parents were away. I suppose Vanessa and I might have attended the same local college and eventually married if it were not for the reckless, deadly turn in our national history.

Amanda Keller had been an especially quiet girl not associated with a set of friends. She seemed to go out of her way not to make friends. At the time I probably thought this was because of politics; almost everything then could be attributed to politics. We lived in an American state that was evenly, exquisitely split between the political parties and our town was split that way too, though certain neighborhoods, ethnic groups, and places of worship were known to fall almost uniformly one way or the other. Our high school was divided along similar lines, and we were easily identifiable according to our styles of dress, haircuts, headwear, shoewear, eyewear, facial hair for the boys, makeup for the girls, music preferences, tattoos, elective classes, school clubs, sport activities, piercings, cars and trucks, drugs and alcohol use, sexual behaviors, and, to some degree, the strides we adopted as we walked the halls. Even those of us who affected obliviousness to politics, like me, knew with which side we were affiliated.

Amanda seemed resolute in not adopting partisan signifiers. Like all of us, she wore jeans to school, but hers were neither prefaded nor vibrantly inked and neither strategically torn nor fully intact. She sometimes wore simple knee-length dresses. There was never anything weird or distinctive going on with her hair—or at least nothing that I would have picked up on, being a guy. Passing through the hallways, she almost seemed to fade into the walls. But reticence could be a form of protest too, or a stance or a statement, even if we weren't sure of its content. I probably assumed that it meant she belonged to the other side and was trying to hide it.

By the autumn of my senior year, when the pace of shootings and other violence across the country had picked up, when the national news was dominated every day by some grave astonishment that made us forget the previous day's astonishment, our school simmered with jaw-clenched anticipation. After a riot in the stands spread onto the field, the football season was canceled. Even our teachers avoided each other, though their profession, like certain other professions, was much less evenly divided. Vanessa and I broke up around then, not over a political disagreement, but because it seemed like the wrong time to maintain attachments or make plans. We limped to finals and graduation, too distracted to care. Militias, paramilitaries, gangs and crews, police auxiliaries, and self-defense groups were establishing themselves.

Membership in one thing or another was getting oblig-
atory. I had really hoped to go to college.

These days I avoided thinking about what had been
lost, the entirety of a way of life that had been composed
of ordinary expectations. This was why I had trained
myself to dwell on happier, rigorously curated thoughts.
By now, however, my day off was just about ruined, even
if the high-altitude clouds had dissipated and an even
more vividly blue sky was emerging. In the strong sun
boys kicked around a ball. I dropped down from the
wall suddenly, as if I could leave my past there. I headed
down the boardwalk. I managed only a few steps. I was
being called to, shouted at.

"Hey! Hey you, hey, you American! Wait!"

I turned. Some woman waved from the other side of
the umbrella shack, smiling broadly. As she approached,
she said, "You're the American, right?"

"Yes," I said, keeping my voice down.

I didn't recognize this person. She was about my
age. She wore white slacks and a blue polo shirt, with
a white nylon windbreaker wrapped around her shoulders like a cape. I warily watched her come down the
boardwalk. People didn't often address me.

"It's me, your hero! I drove the van. Remember?
You asked me to meet you."

Surely I hadn't. Surely she hadn't been the driver. She
didn't look anything like the driver, even supposing that
she might have dressed differently or done something new

with her hair on her day off. Nothing about her, except perhaps her complexion, resembled the woman from the van. I gazed at her, trying to connect her features to the ones I recalled. She met my eyes, merriment playing in them. I now remembered their animation, or something half-similar, from the day of the march. But I had apparently not regained the ability to distinguish one woman from another.

"Right," I said slowly, stupidly. "I didn't think you were coming."

"I know. I'm sorry I'm late." She didn't sound apologetic.

"That's OK. I'm glad you're here," I said, mustering some gallantry. I felt lucky to have a companion, no matter who she was or at what time she arrived, but I remained skeptical.

She told me her name, Marlise, which I said was a pretty name, and we shook hands formally. I thanked her again for the other day. She said her supervisor had laughed when he was told how the airport shuttle had been commandeered. I said I hadn't mentioned the detour to my own supervisor. We looked across the bay for a minute, until she proposed that we take the walk that I had promised. I had forgotten about it. We now made our way along the Corniche in parallel tracks and kept a polite distance from each other, not even grazing shoulders. We were still, of course, strangers. This was not a date, as I had insisted.

Other men and women, more obviously couples, promenaded alongside us and in the opposite direction, some in their holiday clothes, others in beachwear. (I owned neither.) Families were stepping down to the sand with kites and folding chairs. A few of the kites, in designs distinctive to the country, were bobbing in the uneven breeze above the water. We enthused about the weather probably longer than was necessary. I repeated that the Corniche was my favorite place in the city, the place where I felt most at home.

"We have beaches like this in America," I added vaguely, aware that every country with a coastline would have a beach.

She asked me when I left the States. When I told her the year, she wanted to know the month. I told her the names of the countries through which I had sojourned. She took in the information without showing judgment. I told her about my job and where I was headed when I was caught in the protest. I described my living situation, resisting any note of complaint.

At last she said, "This isn't the worst place to end up."

"No," I agreed. "The world is manufacturing worse places every day."

"It has a lovely waterfront," she said and then nodded over her left shoulder. "I like visiting the mountains too. I take the tourist train. The forest is laced with especially complex hiking trails. They say they're so intricate that you can never retrace your steps."

"I've never been," I said. The train was not inexpensive. I added, "I would like to go someday."

She didn't say she would come with me. Instead she said, "Down here in the city, I enjoy the street orchestras."

"Me too," I said. "I've come across them many times. It's amazing how they set up wherever and whenever they like. And those instruments! I don't understand folk music, but I like being in the crowd. Which just kind of materializes."

"It's not any street," she explained. "There are designated places for the concerts and designated times."

"I'm still new here," I conceded.

Farther down the Corniche, a group of older women in flower-patterned one-piece bathing outfits, many of the women heavyset, were doing what I thought was an exercise class on the sand.

"Actually, it's a traditional folk dance," she said, chuckling apologetically. "It's from the southern part of the country."

"Really, there's so much about this place I don't know."

I regretted these admissions. I didn't want to give her the idea that I was incurious. The truth was that I had contact with very few local people, certainly with none who could have introduced me to the country's folk culture. I couldn't afford to dine in restaurants. I often sensed, doing my rounds for work, traveling by foot on the streets and aboard public vehicles, that an impenetrable glass wall lay between me and the city and country in which I was living. Parts of the glass were opaque or smeared or smudged in some way; I could see hardly more than my own reflection, faintly.

An airplane pulled a banner ad over the water. On its second or third pass we read the message: *A MILLION UNEMPLOYED IS A MILLION IMMIGRANTS TOO MANY.*

We didn't speak of it. I was embarrassed and imagined that she was embarrassed for me.

WE CONTINUED TO WALK, trading observations about the city's particular attractions. As we approached the marina, I pointed to a large yacht that I knew belonged to a famous foreign movie actor. We had both seen his films and agreed about several that we liked. Everyone said he had made only a single bomb, I added. Marlise fell silent for a moment, before defending the film with some heat. I argued back fiercely. Then we laughed at our vehemence, though I privately wondered if her praise for such an obviously bad movie was an affectation. We were not, of course, disputing objective facts, but I still found it difficult to believe she could feel the way she said she did.

Even with this trivial disagreement, even with my migrant awkwardness, we seemed very comfortable with each other. It had been years since I had taken part in such an easygoing, aimless conversation.

She asked about America: what state was I from, had I lived in a city or in the country, what kind of work my parents had done, that sort of thing. I described my high school and told her I had played for its baseball team, which she found amusing, though she said she couldn't begin to understand the game. I also told her about the small creek that ran through the community, dividing it demographically, but also supplying us with trout and smallmouth bass. I claimed a favorite fishing spot there, a bend in the river where a century-old oak had tipped over when its root structure became exposed. The part of the riverbed that the tree had lifted from the water had accreted soil and moss into a soft mound, an excellent perch about five feet above the water's surface. I could spend whole days fishing there, but my friends would come to keep me company and then, inevitably, start diving from the mound. That ruined the fishing, of course. Talking about it now, I was almost giddy with pleasure.

She encouraged me to go on with my storytelling, interrupting only to ask for specific details. We reached the busy port area, where the boardwalk was blocked by a security fence. Several lanes of a trolleybus terminus were ranged alongside the customs house. A trolley idled. We both knew that this was a convenient place for her to leave. We looked at the vehicle for a moment. I didn't want to speak of it, or exert any kind of influence, but I didn't want her to go. There was plenty left to

the Sunday. We stood at the fence, watching a container
ship pull out of its berth. Then she turned very deci-
sively, in the direction from where we had come, back up
the Corniche. I went with her.

"Actually," she said. "I arrived at ten. Or five past,
maybe."

She smiled shyly. Now I detected a note of apology
in her tone and behind that a kind of tentativeness, as if
she thought she was taking a consequential step.

"I didn't see you," I protested. "I looked for you!"

"I was hiding."

Now I studied her again, trying to familiarize myself
with the woman's mouth, nose, eyes, hair, and light
makeup. I still didn't recognize her from the day of the
protest march, but I no longer remembered what the
driver looked like.

"Hiding from me?"

"I was standing on the other side of the umbrella
shack. I went behind the porch every time you let yourself down from the wall. I was watching you. I was trying to figure out what kind of person you were, to make
sure you were safe. You know, you can't be too careful
these days."

She was right, the world was increasingly populated
by questionable characters. I encountered them myself,
time and again, to my disadvantage. And my bad hair-
cut and worn loafers couldn't have reassured her. In the
quiet neighborhoods in the old part of the city people

often crossed to the other side of the street when they saw me coming. Yet she hadn't been deterred. The fact that she cared enough to watch me sit on a wall for the better part of an hour suggested an inquisitive nature, but her behavior also embraced an element of strangeness, something akin to her partisanship on behalf of the famous actor's universally derided bad movie.

She said, "Do you mind?"

"I don't know," I said, realizing that her surveillance also indicated at least a sliver of romantic interest. "No, actually, I don't mind at all."

"It's not like you would have known if I hadn't told you," she said, not defensively. "I wasn't hurting you or in any way altering the conditions of your life."

"No, of course not," I said.

"For a while you were very still, gazing into the bay. People passed and you didn't see them. Then you began talking to yourself. Do you do that a lot? It looked like you were telling yourself some kind of story. I couldn't hear it. You were moving your lips and you occasionally did something with your hands as if to emphasize a point. I watched your face. You were sad and then you were angry."

"Jesus."

"That's why I waited so long," she said very seriously. "What was the story about?"

I hadn't realized I had been so unguarded. This was embarrassing, of course, and annoying from several directions. I was irritated at her, but also mad at myself for having so little self-possession, for being so careless. This was also independent confirmation that something was wrong with me and it was getting worse. I thought again of the fear that gripped us all the last year of high school, when we felt the unfairness of everything, the propulsion into a dangerous, hateful adult life for which we weren't close to being prepared. The fear was like a long, serious illness that continued to smolder within my system.

We walked back for a while. It seemed that she was waiting for an answer. I considered several responses, each another story, each contradicting the other and a few that were especially painful. Finally, I simply said, "America."

She nodded. I appreciated this small, rare gesture of sympathy.

At the fishing pier an elderly woman with a bright, grooved face occupied a stool. We stopped to look at her bucket of porgies. She gazed at us with a warmth that suggested she thought we were a couple. Now, seeing us in the old woman's eyes, my new acquaintance represented a multitude of possibilities. Perhaps Marlise would be my guide to the city and to the rest of the country as well. I would try the local cuisine. I was being excessively optimistic, of course. I watched the fish splashing in the pail. I hadn't put a line in the water since I left the States.

"You know," Marlise said lightly. "I'm not from here either."

I laughed, forgiving her for her wariness. I wasn't familiar enough with the local language, the one in which we were speaking, to have detected her accent. She named her native country, which was located on a distant continent. This country had also been roiled by political turmoil for most of the past decade and it too had sent many young people abroad.

"I was about to attend the national university," she said. "The art history program. But there's no university anymore. What's left of the campus is occupied by soldiers. The museum's probably been looted."

Marlise said she had lived in this city for several years now. She had recently begun working for the airport shuttle company. It was not a bad job even if, as a migrant, she was paid next to nothing. Several times a day she returned to the airport at which she had arrived, but she said she never allowed herself the fantastic, self-indulgent thought that she was on her way home. She occasionally picked up passengers who spoke her language among themselves. She never revealed herself to them. She didn't want to get into anything like a political conversation or, since the divisions in her country had only deepened, something worse.

THAT AFTERNOON, ONCE WE reached the end of the Corniche where we started, near the umbrella shack, we shook hands again. I waited, hoping she would say we could get together again. She didn't. I was hoping, now that it was shown that our residency statuses were comparable, that I would find a way to call our next meeting a date. I didn't. I told her I would come back to this place on my next day off the following Sunday, unless it rained. She said all right, perhaps she would meet me. Sunday was her regular day off too.

I couldn't help myself. "But this was agreeable, right?"

The local language, like many of the world's languages, had no word for "fun" in the American sense. The word probably no longer had an American sense either.

"It was OK." She smiled lightly.

"Don't watch me next time," I said. "I'm not putting on any more shows."

"If you can help it."

She arrived the following Sunday and most of the Sundays after that, always a few minutes after I did, and I could never abandon the thought that she had been spying. She called my name from a distance, gaily, but from near a bus shelter or a kiosk from which she could have obscured herself. Then it took a moment for me to familiarize myself with her. Every time she adopted a slightly different look, in pants or a sundress or a skirt, her hair worn up or down or parted or bobbed, her lipstick in a new shade or unapplied. But then I knew it was her. During the week, elsewhere in the city, I stopped thinking I recognized her or women who looked like her. My mind seemed to have settled on this woman alone, as if the curse of clouded vision was slowly lifting.

Some days we packed sandwiches and ate lunch on the benches at the edge of the beach. Marlise enjoyed watching the small children chase each other, fly kites, and make sandcastles. When a loose ball bounced onto the Corniche near us, she kicked or threw it back to them with obvious feeling. She then smiled in a way that I thought might be more transparent than the way she smiled at me.

"It may be hard to believe now," she said, "but my city was once one of the continent's major capitals. Our people were educated, humane, and cosmopolitan. We had shops and restaurants far more fashionable than anything in this country. Yet it was also a homey, authentic place, where everyone knew each other or at least each other's cousin or cousin's cousin. At the outdoor markets, which were famously raucous, you'd find the most delicious cheeses and other local foods. It's all destroyed now."

"I'm sorry. I knew about your country. I thought I might travel there someday, like on vacation."

"There was a certain kind of savory pastry," she said, pronouncing the name. "I could never get enough of them, even if it meant ruining my dinner. Migrants sell them here from street carts, but the crust is never right. And you inevitably get a harangue about the war."

But she mostly turned the conversation toward

America, which was still a nation that held great interest for people around the globe, even if their curiosity had turned to morbid fascination. Had Americans in my town been rich or poor? Had people from her country settled there? Had they been rich? Had there been cinemas? How were women treated? What were my friends like? Did I have a girlfriend? Did I have a dog? She especially wanted to know about our high school, the number of students, what time the day started, the color of the tiles that lined the hallways, even the distinctively American names of the teachers.

I could speak with great enthusiasm about the place, which I continued to revisit in my imagination. I spoke of my hometown with her as I would have described it to any foreign person who was interested. I was probably pedantic and I may have belabored the former fine points of American life, like the independent judiciary. She listened attentively, her head tilted, her eyes in the distance, as if she were taking mental notes.

The streets of the city where she said she came from were vividly described, but there was always a significant part of my consciousness, deep in the back of my head, that believed—correctly, as I would recognize years later—that she was not being truthful about who she was. Untruthfulness was not unusual. In that age of turmoil and flight many people assumed new identities, provided they could acquire the corresponding documentation. They would make up new life stories and stick to them. It was impolite to express doubt. It would have also challenged the growing warmth between us. I occasionally caught her reflection in a shopwindow or an automobile windshield and I held the image in mind. The casualness of our company eventually started to seem artificial, for these walks were obviously something we looked forward to for more than the exercise. At some point we started kissing each other when we met and parted, a custom that was typical of this city but not of the small-town America in which I had grown up; my vagueness about when it began is facetious, because I know perfectly well, as well as my shoe size, the exact date and time of day, down to the lightning hour and minute, when she leaned in to brush my cheek. She smiled a little wistfully at my surprise. I would look forward to our next meeting. Otherwise we were careful to limit our affections, knowing that the unreliability of our residency permissions made courtship too perilous. We walked side by side and apart, friendly and reserved, our conversation candid but carefully constructed, even if I was keenly sensitive to the sway of her hips, etc.

We sometimes left the Corniche to explore other sections of the sprawling city whose cartography I was very familiar with from my job, but which in her company unfolded in unexpected ways. We stopped at market stalls and food trucks. Every street turned newly significant, generating a history as a place where we had been together. I might later recall some specific words exchanged on any block, or a smile or a frown, or a corner at which our bodies inadvertently touched or perhaps not so inadvertently. The city on the bay soon became for me two very distinct metropolises, one where I did my inspections and maintenance, and a second city, overlaid upon it, across which we rambled for hours at a time.

Like me, Marlise reported six days a week to her regular job. She also had evening babysitting work, women from her country being especially prized as caregivers. But when she told me that she loved kids, her intonation was oddly flat. She also mentioned that she lived in a tiny apartment. I went out of my way not to ask in which neighborhood and she never volunteered the information.

On Sundays when the weather was bad, I usually went to the public library's reading room, a marbled rotunda in the center of a historic centuries-old building, and Marlise sometimes met me, though she never promised that she would. Without violating the library's injunction against conversation, she took a place on the other side of the inlaid mahogany table. Our books were opened beneath reading lamps housed in lime-green glass shades. I would read a novel published in English, drawn from the library's vast holdings that were collected when English was the world's most popular second language. Marlise would look at a large-format locally published art book. She still hoped to study art someday. I gazed at her as she read, trying to fix in my mind how I would remember her.

✦

The new residency rules that were announced were far more severe than anyone had anticipated, a political masterstroke that left the government's nativist opponents sputtering in rage but without an argument. Not only were new migrants barred from entering the country—in a year when millions of people were on the move, some washing up dead on the country's shores, some right here in the bay—recent arrivals like me and Marlise would have to leave once the executive order was put into place. The list of countries that still accepted migrants was rapidly dwindling. Every one of us studied the list's fine print to determine where he or she could find at least a temporary home, and with what papers.

The skies gathering around the Sunday that followed the executive order promised rain and I almost decided not to go to the Corniche, especially since I didn't think Marlise would come, but then I thought perhaps she would. I descended from my tram at precisely ten. I saw that she had arrived before me, for the first time in the months since we began walking together. She stood by the wall near the umbrella shack, her back to me, about fifty meters away.

I didn't hide, but I approached in small steps, watching her wait. I could see her only from behind, and again I wasn't sure it was her, but I thought that by this time I could recognize the contours of her jeaned lower body, and also the raincoat over her shoulders. These few moments of private observation were rare, allowing me to interrogate her physical self, the woman. Her ankles below the cuffs of her pants. The sweep of her bare neck. Whatever were the necessary parameters of our friendship, I took relish in these things.

The light this morning was odd, harsher and at the same time duller than usual, a kind of penetrating gray. The bay's waters had turned greenish and waves lapped at the beach, bringing reports of storms elsewhere, and in fact world events had taken a turn for the worse: a disputed election, a coup, a many-sided war. Some stiff-legged seabirds picked in the filthy sand, which was otherwise unpopulated.

"Marlise!" I cried.

When she turned I thought I had committed the kind of mistake I hadn't made in a while. It was Marlise, but I didn't immediately identify her, because I had never seen her face creased like this, reflective of the disturbances in the atmosphere.

"Hello, Ron," she said quietly.

"Hey," I said. I gave her a questioning look.

She didn't respond, but she took off down the Corniche, walking fast, almost as if she were trying to get away from me, but that wasn't it. She was trying to leave the place where she had been waiting, again the locus of unhappy thoughts. I kept up with her for a few minutes. She stopped abruptly.

"Where am I going to go?" she demanded. "Where are you going? Not back to the States, are you?"

"That's impossible. I don't want to fight. I don't want to be killed. There aren't any jobs anyway."

We slowed to a more contemplative pace. More people had come out to the boardwalk, families with children, a gaggle of teenage girls, couples on tandem bicycles— happier people, I thought. Legal residents. The city's entire migrant population must have been brooding about its next step that morning.

"Things are just as bad in my country," Marlise said. "The government holds most of the capital, but it's been bombing the suburbs for years. Barrel bombs, poison gas: whole neighborhoods have been obliterated. People have starved to death, you've seen pictures of the malnourished kids. And we have internment camps too."

"Ours are bigger," I said. This was an American-style joke.

She named several countries that might accept her passport and give her a temporary visa. These were nations that had either a historic relationship with hers or nations with which her country was currently in opposition. I speculated too about which countries might plausibly find me eligible for a provisional residency. None of our countries matched, unsurprisingly.

I took a wild chance. I said, haltingly, "I wonder if we were married . . . You know, as a convenience . . . Maybe there'll be new visa options . . . Of course, everyone's cracking down on that. It's probably impossible."

She didn't respond and I felt my face warm.

We walked for a while. We passed the marina and I murmured that the famous actor's yacht had left. Yachts left regularly, but since the political crisis began many wealthy foreign people had departed the country for good. The actor was technically a migrant too, and even if he had the means to buy himself legal residency, he might have been unsettled by the change in the social climate.

To break the silence, I said, "Not that I could ever marry anyone who liked that movie."

"I'm already married."

There was some weakness in my knees, but I kept up with her. What I felt mostly was anger at my surprise and at the indwelling foolishness that continued to track me across the globe. Marlise had always been guarded about her private life. I should have figured there was something she wasn't telling me. Another guy would have been the most likely candidate.

"Congratulations," I said, aiming for lightness. "Who's the lucky fellow?"

She shrugged. "He's not so lucky. He's still in my country. He was in the resistance and then he was in something pro-regime, or maybe it was the other way around. The sides keep gaining and losing ground, loyalties shift, even he couldn't keep it straight. He was studying literature when I met him, just out of high school, just as things were falling apart. I thought he was sophisticated, kind of an intellectual. He liked fancy cars, good restaurants, long theoretical talks with friends. Not an obvious soldier. He did, however, have a terrible temper, a kind of mad rage that was triggered by every frustration. So that came in use when they gave him a gun. He loved having a gun. I don't know where he is now. Maybe he's in prison. That's probably the safest place for him."

I said, lamely, "I'm sorry."

She shook her head. "It was more difficult for men to leave, but he could have gone."

"Why didn't he?"

"He said he could handle the situation." She shrugged. "Really, he loved the gun. He didn't want to give it up."

We walked for a while and she added, "I had stopped thinking about him, almost. It would be better if I stopped thinking about him. He was a dream. It would be better if I stopped thinking of the place I came from. It's a dream too, a hallucination, a false memory, a race memory, a story I tell myself. Maybe every homeland, every home, is a story, always. *This* is my home now." She waved at the city on the other side of the Corniche, the stone buildings and the glass towers taking on varying shades of the day's gray light. She extended an arm toward the mountains and then swept it down to the bay. "This is the story that seems real to me now."

When we reached the fence at the Navy Yard she said she would catch a tram from there, something she had done only once or twice before. She seemed very fatigued. She saw that I was disappointed, and asked me to walk her to the stop.

The vehicle was already there, the driver standing outside at the front of it, finishing a cigarette. Marlise wished me luck searching for a new country in which to live. Again she made no promise that she would see me the following Sunday. The driver flicked the butt onto the pavement. Marlise kissed my cheek, lingering for a moment, and said, "Ron, you seem real too."

"I'm glad I do. All this to-ing and fro-ing . . ." I manufactured a laugh. "Living out of a small suitcase, packing and unpacking it as if its contents matter, as if they truly represent who we are. Acquaintances coming and going and forgetting. We never leave a trace. It's not exactly an actual existence. I sometimes think I'm no more than my documents, just a passport and a collection of stamps. The wrong stamps."

Marlise said she and her husband had a son. He would be seven now.

The "would be" gave me a start.

She looked away. She said that once the fighting began, children were taken from the combatants for their own protection. Some parents resisted. Force had to be used. The kids were put on buses to facilities in safer parts of the country. It had been a chaotic time. Social agencies were understaffed and underfunded and they were overwhelmed by the number of children involved. Records were poorly kept or lost or corrupted. Some of the infants and toddlers were evidently misplaced. Marlise had no idea what happened to her son, or even whether he had ever attended school. For a moment, this last thought seemed about to overwhelm her, but the tram's electric motor buzzed on, and she climbed into the vehicle.

✦

Marlise didn't come the following Sunday, probably as brilliant a day as the Corniche had ever enjoyed. She wasn't there the next week either and I waited a full hour at the umbrella stand. Meanwhile, as the days that I would be permitted to stay in the country slipped away, I scrambled to find refuge. During the week I took off from my job to join lines at embassies and consuls, or at nongovernmental migrant assistance offices. The same paperwork was filled out time and again. The migrant assistance offices were open on Sundays, but I didn't want to give up those days if there was a chance that I would see Marlise.

As much as I could be sure of anything, I believed

she wouldn't leave without saying goodbye, unless an urgent, time-limited opportunity presented itself. This was not impossible. Doors swung open and then they slammed shut. I could imagine myself leaving suddenly too, though I hoped not to go before seeing her, even as I became increasingly desperate. No one wanted Americans that year.

So I was relieved a few weeks later, when I had almost given up hope. She was again waiting for me on the Corniche, this time watching as I came off the tram. She smiled coolly, inviting me to guess what the smile was about. I was surprised when her face loomed into my line of sight and she kissed me directly on the lips. It happened very quickly, the moment receding at light speed. She laughed at my wonderment, but I knew what it meant. She named her destination. I was impressed. This was a nation with a robust economy, the rule of law, and a thriving local culture. Its harsh climate was a minor annoyance. I had gone to this country's embassy a month ago but, once I showed my American passport, I wasn't allowed through the front gate. Marlise's direct flight would leave in three weeks. The taste of her lips remained on mine.

"You'll get residency somewhere," she said excitedly. "I'm sure you will!"

"I hope so."

"Or something like residency."

"There are all kinds of travel and residence permits

out there," I agreed, trying not to think of all those I had been refused. "Many categories of traveler."

We talked about all the places I might go, exotic lands and capitals of culture. Some of these countries might have good, decent-paying jobs. We also spoke of our time in the city together, on the Corniche and in the library. We replayed some of our favorite excursions: to the vast outdoor secondhand electronics market, to the public gardens, and to the mountains, where we were once very briefly separated on the trails. We embraced when we found each other, deeply relieved. Even as we were being expelled, the city was transforming itself into a reminiscence about another distant place.

Now we walked to the Navy Yard, and at the end of the Corniche, without discussing where we were going, we turned toward downtown, first passing through the historic former industrial area that was fitfully being converted into a loft district. We crossed the commercial avenue where she had rescued me. I was being led. We went by the library. On another block dim, cluttered shops sold used wood furniture that wasn't good enough to be called antiques. We looked into the windows for a while. A massive oak bookcase appealed to me as something I would like to have someday, if only for its immovability. In the crimson afternoon light, the wood looked on the verge of igniting.

We entered a quiet, residential street of gray stone apartment buildings that were still handsome, if a little shabby. She stopped suddenly halfway down the block. This building leaned further on the shabby side: boards blocked a ground-floor window, chunks of the pediment were gone. I wondered why we stopped. The sky had changed, anticipating dusk. Strangers passed us on the street. Marlise asked if I would like to come up. She wasn't smiling and her meaning was clear. I raised my head, showing confusion, as if she were asking me to climb the outside of the building.

"You live here?"

"For a few more weeks."

"How long have you lived here?"

Now it was her turn to be puzzled. It was an odd question, at least for the moment. She must have thought I was stalling. I may have been stalling, even if the invitation was long desired.

"For a while," she said, with a shrug. "It's cheap." Then she clarified: "For years, ever since I came to this country."

We were far from the neighborhood where I had seen the woman in the rooftop flat. I had not, of course, forgotten the incident. Her image had vanished into the mists, but the fog wasn't thick enough to conceal the possibility, nurtured on the thinnest of hopes, that Marlise and the woman were the same person. As I walked alongside her on our Sundays together I had never lost awareness of this potential, which simmered beneath her clothes, her body shifting and straining against the fabric. I imagined that I had already seen those naked legs and buttocks that were propelling this corporeal self down the Corniche.

This evening, on the street in front of the building where she really lived, I experienced an immediate letdown. I was surprised to discover how much of my sexual imagination had linked Marlise to my act of trespass on the roof. Romantic desire had been invested in this notion too, assumed from my possession of secret knowledge and secret intimacy, even if I hardly remembered the barely glimpsed woman, who was now completely dematerialized. The incident no longer felt like something that had really happened.

We kissed in the dim, creaky, urine-dank elevator, but tentatively, searching for signs in each other's eyes, and by the pressure of our lips, to be sure that this was what we wanted from each other. I had been sure before. Now I was reminded how much my idea of this woman had been a projection of whom I wanted her to be—but what object of romance was not?—and that I knew her only from the stories she told me. But what else can we know of each other? And what else can we know of the places we live or the lands we came from? These stories had been selected and edited, as they always were. They had elided several details, as usual. I had never fully believed them anyway. So who did I think I was kissing?

Her apartment was small, as she had said, with only enough room for a narrow futon. I must have looked at it with concern. She said we'd manage. When I embraced her again I became aware just how deeply buried, how denied, my yearning for her, whoever she was, had been. It rose to the surface now with a force that electrified every nerve. Whatever the initial disappointment, my eagerness and my excitement were augmented by relief that the secret offense that I had committed months ago had not been performed against this person.

We had been shy with each other, but now I was astounded by the fact and the miracle of her physical manifestation. So these are her breasts, this is her ass. I couldn't recall whether the hidden parts of her body were precisely how I had expected them to be, in shape or size or whatever. She may have wondered about the expression of my bewilderment, a series of happy, childish giggles.

We'd meet almost every evening of the remaining weeks, whenever we were free of other obligations, which mostly had to do with organizing our departures. We toured the remaining unexplored neighborhoods of the city but always ended up here, in her flat. Every time I was startled by the bareness of her skin; also by the intensity of her attention.

Thus I tried to segregate every encounter in my recall, keeping distinct each kiss, each caress, and the words we exchanged. She knew about my determined memory-keeping and she would jokingly ask about something that happened or that we did the time before last. I told her and she would say she remembered it or that she didn't, but I understood that she intended to remember it too: a souvenir of this time and place. As much gratification as I gathered in, also to be stored and carried away, I was disconcerted by the extent of her hunger and her need, of which I hadn't been aware. I was unconvinced that it had to do with the conventional ingredients of romantic desire; it was rather more like a question to which she was urgently demanding an answer. The question had to do with two people occupying the present moment in this present city. The question may have also been about the past, about what she had brought here with her, about who she really was.

In any case, the question would not have been about the future. The only thing that had changed between us was her new visa.

After we entered her flat, she usually removed her contact lenses. I'd watch her carefully, step by step. She never replaced them with glasses.

✦

Our days together were running out. I finally received a tourist visa from a remote country, far from the place that was offering Marlise her provisional home.

The afternoon before she left she ran some last-minute errands and we met on the Corniche just as evening fell, when the waterfront acquired hues, shades, sounds, and a personality with which we weren't familiar. We had never been here at this hour before. We walked among fresh sets of vendors, buskers, and watercolorists who had uncapped paints of novel tints. The water of the bay was still and opaque. In this purpling light I came to feel that I had never really come to know my favorite place in the city; this uncertainty seemed to extend to my knowledge of Marlise. I gazed at her and again there was a moment of nonrecognition. I wondered if I would ever have another opportunity to not recognize her.

We walked along the bay to the Navy Yard. Weeks ago she had stopped asking me about the United States. Now we were trading what little we knew about the countries to which we would be traveling, trying to imagine our new lives, though we didn't speak of being apart or whether we would miss each other. My multi-segmented discount flight to the other side of the world was scheduled the following week. From the Navy Yard we walked across the city, through neighborhoods rich in dinner fragrances, my anticipation making me talk hurriedly and forcefully. I didn't know where we were or by what roundabout way we arrived at her building in the early morning hours. We ascended to her room. Her few things were packed in a single beige suitcase that was placed in the center of the uncarpeted floor.

Early that morning we dozed off on the futon, her warm and damp body half on mine, a light blanket covering us both. When I dreamed, it was to reprise our coupling. I woke well before her, aroused, as the rising sun just started to add shape and color to the room. I gazed at her face, every line and crease in stark relief, marks of her time in the city. Her eyes flickered open eventually.

"What? You're still here?"

I told her that I loved her. She took in this confession calmly, almost as a matter of course. I added that she had made the city a livable place for me, more than livable. Here in this room, with her, regardless of the lasting orthopedic problems I would suffer from her sleeping surface, I felt the closest I had come to being at home. I told her that I felt I had known her for a long time, from well before I met her, and that she would always be close to my heart. I admitted, abashedly, that I couldn't get out of my mind the idea that she was actually American.

"Do you mean like that girl from your high school? With the nice name?"

"Amanda."

"You still think I'm her?"

"Not really," I said.

She asked me to reach next to the suitcase for her knapsack carry-on. I pulled it toward the bed. She told me to open the zipper in the outer compartment. I removed a ruby-red passport, to which was stapled another document, the precious visa for her new country.

"Open the book to the first page."

The passport was issued to Marlise Larijani by her country of birth, which was now being pulverized on one side by the central government and on the other by several competing separatist armies. Her name was printed there, along with the names of her parents, her birth date, her place of birth, and the date and place the passport was issued. These place-names, once signifying localities remote, historic, and strangely picturesque, had recently become synonyms for atrocity.

Despite my weeks of fondling her solid flesh and being enveloped by it, breathing in her sour and sweet odors, and pressing against her lips and other soft parts, I discovered a new level of physicality in the document's alphanumerics. Boilerplate official language, cursively inscribed, attested to the passport's power and the reality of its bearer. Stamps on several pages demonstrated that this realness had been accepted by uniformed men and women at several airports and other legal points of entry.

The picture, however, looked nothing like her. It would have been taken years ago, when the passport was applied for, but even so the person photographed and laminated was more like a schoolgirl, with bangs and an embarrassed toothy grin, and with her features sized not quite in the familiar proportions. I looked at the woman resting her head on my shoulder, smiling up at me, perhaps mischievously and knowing, or perhaps bitterly sad, and I closed the document. I wondered how well trained they were at her new country's passport control.

I put it back in the carry-on, shoving it alongside an eyeglass case I had never seen before.

She snorted at me, perhaps for doubting her, perhaps for being so gullible. She lightly touched me under the cover.

"It was just a fantasy," I insisted, my insistence not entirely sincere. "I never really believed it. This has been such a confusing time. Disorienting. Right? Every migrant is disoriented, out of place, unsure of his footing, unsure about the basic elements of his new reality. You know, when I first started walking with you on the Corniche, I didn't recognize you from one walk to the next. Every time I saw you, it was a surprise." Trying to make it sound romantic, I added, "A happy surprise."

Then I explained how there had been another woman, before we met, who I had come to believe was her. I told her how I had seen this woman leaving her shower while I was on the roof of a building where I was doing maintenance, a certain address on a well-known street on the north side of the city, and also how I had not left right away, though I could have. I told her that I thought I had gotten a good look at her—and I certainly had taken my time—but I could no longer remember her face or form. There had been times when I thought she and this woman were the same person.

Marlise was less amused than I expected her to be. I thought, perhaps incorrectly, that I detected a cooling of her skin against mine or a stiffening of her body, or something like that. I was about to elaborate on what I had observed that afternoon, playing the scene for laughs, but now I found myself abbreviating what was after all a trivial anecdote. She had removed her hand.

"A voyeur! A deviant! I had no idea," she joked, but the response seemed forced.

"In English we say 'Peeping Tom.' That's no compliment either."

"Peeping Tom," she repeated. "Disgusting! Do you do a lot of that in America?"

I was puzzled by the possibility that she had taken offense. She was an experienced and inventive lover— and boldly direct in her demands. In the past couple of weeks we had been sexually intimate in every conceivable way, some of them strange to me. A few of the things we did, which make my mouth dry when I think of them now, many cultures would have found much more unsavory than taking a clandestine look at someone who was unclothed. But as I heard myself tell the story for the first time, I was becoming aware of how embarrassingly unseemly my spying had been. Or at least I was seeing how it might have been considered unseemly by someone else.

The moment for renewed lovemaking had passed and she had a plane to catch. We still had to make our farewells, which were affectionate and regretful, no promises being possible. We embraced. Yet even as I took one last kiss, a gentle touch on her lips, and she gazed at me as she closed the door, I felt that something awkward, one last thing, had come between us.

II

In my next country of residence no one believed I was a tourist, not at the airport when I arrived nor when I looked for places to live and work. It was hard to find work and then once I did, in a food-processing plant, I overstayed my visa, until I couldn't any longer. Further crackdowns were coming. I went to another country and then another after that, each move a last-minute escape from a looming migrant center or prison. One desert border was crossed on foot with about a dozen other undocumented travelers of diverse origins, led by smugglers who did not know the way as well as advertised. The noonday frigidity broke records, yet in its lack of relief, its desolation, its stillness, and its boundless, cloudless, birdless sky, the desert was a place of strange and absolute beauty. Every one of the desperate migrants was aware of this beauty, this gorgeousness, this transcendence, this manifestation of perfect harmony, as if it were a discrete, substantial item, its appreciation the full purpose of human existence, even as we suffered for it. We continued on, watching our steps. Night fell, the cold like a blade slicing through every inch of our exposed skin, and a family with an elderly parent had to be left behind, still drinking in the beauty.

For ten months or so I belonged to a crew on a container ship flying a flag of convenience. My passport wouldn't allow me ashore in most ports. The borderless, visa-free ocean was my home.

The American catastrophe had meanwhile entered a new phase that drained the world of any cruel pleasure it had taken in our downfall. Now the overwhelming sentiment was pity. I followed the news with averted eyes.

Around the same time, the technology used to monitor international travel and border security had matured into an airtight system, employing biometric indicators and closely networked databases. A cashless, digital economy and location services embedded into nearly every electronic device made it possible for any nation to know the identity and whereabouts of every last person within its borders and determine his or her residency status, legal or not. Unsanctioned migration had become virtually impossible.

Either for reasons of compassion, domestic politics, or workforce considerations, or a combination of the three, a few nations continued to accept migrant Americans. One of these, my new refuge, was a country with which the United States had few historic connections. Its principal ethnic group had never been a component of our celebrated melting pot. Its people, in turn, were mostly unfamiliar with American history, our culture, our mores, and our skin tones. Surprised salesclerks would stare when we entered their shops. Beyond linguistic specialists at the university, very few local people spoke English and the national language's non-Indo-European roots, labyrinthine grammar, and subtle intonation system made it very difficult for us to learn. I was good at acquiring foreign languages, but I would pick up only enough for a simple conversation.

We were tolerated, though. Americans came to occupy a vast enclave on the broad marshy plain outside the capital city. Obsolete industrial buildings, abandoned data-processing and call centers, landfills, and dumps sprawled across the territory. At one time the area had been settled by workers who had come from the country's hinterlands and laid down blocks upon blocks of bungalows, shacks, tenements, and smoky, huddled family compounds. They left and years later Americans moved in, showing some ingenuity in improving living conditions. The newcomers jury-rigged water, sewage, and electrical systems, not always safely or in conformity with government standards, which, in this outlying quarter, were laxly observed. The congestion of the streets, the ramshackleness of the residential structures and improvisational dwellings, their confines, the noise and refuse, and the limited penetration of daylight were beyond most of the Americans' experience.

But when I first arrived I was struck by how familiar or semi-familiar the enclave seemed. Some effort had been expended to make the neighborhood more homelike, even if the style of the buildings and the materials used in paving the streets and sidewalks were utterly native to this country. Unofficial signage was posted in English alongside the local undifferentiable squiggles. The principal street was lined with hamburger shops and frozen yogurt stores, some of which assumed vintage American brand names and a limited version of their former signage and trade dress. The enclave was usually identified by a tortuously anglicized rendering of its original, unpronounceable name. No one called it Little America, but that's how it was thought of by its inhabitants, or at least that's how I thought of it.

I soon learned that the Americans had also imported their divisions. This was inevitable, I suppose. None of our divisions had been erased. The circumstances of living together in a single enclave, however, made it difficult to isolate the political sides geographically, as they were often separated in the States. Some buildings, some neighborhoods, and some places of business went one way or another, unpredictably, but we basically lived on top of each other. This resulted in a constant low-grade insecurity, a buzzing tension. The parties no longer had a country to fight over, so the former paramilitaries had reassembled themselves into criminal gangs still affiliated with their political convictions, even if those convictions were irrelevant in this new place and barely recalled. You'd see their men around, everywhere.

Shortly after I arrived, while I was exhausting my money at a primitive boardinghouse, I went for a long walk through the district, trying to get my bearings. The streets were full. People wore their clothes in the American style and their faces were recognizably American. They addressed each other in English, with familiar regional accents. It was a relief to hear the language spoken, especially by small children, most of whom, I guessed, hadn't been born in the States. Passing a small factory that had been turned into a primary school, I heard a familiar jump rope rhyme in the yard. If I closed my eyes, I might have thought I was home, for a few moments at least, before being disabused by everything else that was strange about the place. On the main shopping avenue, a hamburger restaurant called itself by the name of the most famous American hamburger brand, which had gone out of business years earlier. The custom-made signage wasn't quite right and neither were the indoor furnishings, which attempted to replicate the überfamiliar furnishings of the original. They too had to be made from scratch, of course, or scavenged from unrelated local businesses. I ordered a burger. I was stunned by how expensive it was and how nasty, nothing like the hamburgers I thought I enjoyed. Fries were unavailable.

Back on the street, I realized that many food and retail outlets had adopted retired brand names, in some cases the names of businesses unrelated to the items they were selling. A sporting-goods store had taken on the name of a former supermarket chain; an auto-repair shop called itself after a popular jeans brand, with an attempt at the jeans brand's logo in the signage. The names had evidently been chosen because the brands had once meant something. They had each expressed a specific outlook about the world and we considered our purchases acts of self-expression. In those days, in America, one might have assigned a specific character to a person, quite reliably, by where he or she shopped and by the brands he or she valued. You could probably tell how he or she voted. Men with guns could tell too.

✦

Soon after I arrived I was hired to inspect the same kind of security equipment that I had serviced in the city on the bay nearly a decade earlier. My employers were pleased with my experience and my proficiency, especially as it was difficult to find native-born repairmen comfortable with working in the enclave. No major changes had been made in the equipment's design. The only difference in the job was that the units, installed all over the world on the roofs of buildings, were almost invariably placed in the enclave's basements and subbasements. This may have had something to do with the unenforced building codes. I was given a powerful flashlight and advised to wear thick boots.

I bought a bicycle, which I used to make service calls in all weather. A car was well out of my reach, as it was for most migrants who were not involved in criminal activity. Many were. Reunited in exile, the former militiamen now operated off-the-books enterprises, like moving drugs and running casinos, which seemed like the enclave's most viable businesses. I'd see the men descending from their sport utility vehicles, often accompanied by security escorts. They paid no attention to me as I biked past and I made an effort to show that I wasn't paying attention to them, and that in fact I hadn't seen them at all.

The national government to some extent also ignored the former fighters and their new vocations, seemingly content with its limited writ in the enclave. Officials didn't mind that a few vendettas had been carried over from the States and that the former militias remained intensely competitive, as long as everything was kept among the Americans. I presumed some payoffs were involved, but obviously this was none of my business.

MY JOB SATISFIED ME, even if my work was now conducted mostly underground. Every balky control unit represented a unique puzzle, a gratifying intellectual challenge that I was good at solving. I liked bicycling through the enclave. It was colorful and lively and intensely American, though anything resembling these particular streets and structures would never have been found in the States. I came to know some residents and their children. They recognized my company uniform and welcomed my presence as something official and benign, a rare combination in the enclave, where there was no mail delivery and few other public services. I waved at the children with my flashlight.

Sometimes the kids only stared and I wondered if they were reporting my itinerary to the militias, who I supposed kept close tabs on what was happening within the district. I thought I could sense this surveillance, even though it was very surreptitious, and close to imperceptible, and possibly a figment of my imagination. Some buildings I entered were controlled by one gang or another. A few streets were no-go areas for the other gangs. So people could have been interested in my travels, what I saw, what I knew. I could not be sure *how* I was being watched, but the surveillance was not a figment, I thought with some confidence, or at least with as much confidence as I could ever muster—no less aware, after these many years of dislocation, that I was susceptible to impossible fancies and radical uncertainty.

From time to time I was sent outside the enclave to inspect rooftop equipment in the downtown business district, which had recently become the continent's most important financial capital. Audacious new construction dwarfed the pretensions of the other cities in which I had lived. Whole neighborhoods had been razed and rebuilt and they were now serviced by sleek, superfast public transport, stylish bistros, and high-end retail shops. Sharp-looking businesspeople from all over the region flooded the granite sidewalks. In the new skyscrapers, aerodynamically advanced elevators zoomed me more than a hundred stories above the landscape, where the enclave was barely discoverable among the city's outlying territories.

Recalling an earlier architectural style, the new buildings were walled by towering sheets of glass, some of it highly reflective. Decorative and artistic objects in the plazas, situated around perfectly still wading pools, were surfaced in stainless steel. Some objects were concave shaped, others convex, fabricated with a variety of focal lengths. The result for the observer, walking determinedly from one corporate complex to the other, was a cacophony of reflected images, some of them distorted or unexpectedly located, chunks of sidewalk or passing buses flying above his head or patches of sky scurrying by his feet.

Many of the images were generated by my own self, so that I was always accompanied on my travels to the city, under my own surveillance. Copies of Ron Patterson and his toolbox echoed between the mirrored surfaces ad infinitum. But they weren't precise copies, probably because of something having to do with the surface optics, and they often made him look older or thinner, more American or less so, less worn or more athletic, smarter or less lonely, suggesting the other fellows that were contained within him, the fellows that could have been him, if events had turned out differently.

✦

Compared to the skyscraper rooftops, which were noiseless save for the winds, the enclave's basements were as clamorous as train stations, kindergartens, and football stadiums. First, I would often hear the sound of other people speaking and moving elsewhere in the building. And then the structures creaked, water dripped, rats skittered just beyond the reach of my light, the country's indigenous cockroaches made little tap-tap-tap noises, and there were always a few other sounds I couldn't identify. Plus, occasionally, I heard a human step very close, a shuffle, a breath, whatever emanations might signify a human presence. I'd put on a friendly, harmless smile while I waited for the person to appear. There was nobody . . .

. . . until there was. This time I hadn't heard a thing. I was in a small alcove in a subbasement, closing the panel of a unit I had just inspected. As I turned, a bulky figure presented itself and occupied virtually the entire doorway. This must have given me a start, but I quickly recovered.

"Hi, how are you?" I said in the local language. "I'm just finishing up here, everything checks out."

The light was so poor that I could hardly see the man's face or its expression. But he was obviously a native person. He gazed at me. Then he looked down at a pocket-size notebook.

"You're Ron Patterson, I believe," he said in heavily accented English. "An American."

"Yes, sir," I said. I told him whom I worked for.

He nodded, confirming this with whatever was written in his notebook.

The man didn't say anything for a while. His presence seemed to expand until it filled every space in the room. I couldn't get past him, of course.

He finally spoke, staying in English with some difficulty. He told me that he was a police detective. He told me his name, a random assortment of affricates and diphthongs that I couldn't possibly retain. He said he was assigned to the enclave, which I guessed from his manner was an unhappy assignment, perhaps a demotion. He was sent here because he spoke some English. He said his mother had been Irish, though I observed nothing about his features that were remotely Irish. He was responsible for the safety of American migrants, he explained. This declaration would have come off as idealistic or even pompous if his command of the language had been more confident.

He was, I thought, a sad and awkward person. I had

no doubt about his bulk, however, and his capacity to throw it around, if necessary. Although the police in this country didn't commonly carry guns, he reserved the other prerogatives attached to the police of most countries. And, perhaps, in this rough neighborhood, he did indeed carry a gun.

"You need to help me," he said, his words sinking into my gut like one of the hamburgers. "You have a responsibility. You have to protect your people."

"What people?"

"The American people," he intoned, sounding like an American politician, except for the nearly confounding accent and mispronunciation. "You can go anywhere in the district, any building. Good. Continue with your inspections. But you need to open your eyes and ears. Tell me what the gangs are doing, what they're planning. I have to know about any kind of conflict that might happen. I'm here to save American lives."

Aware that my permission to live in his country was revocable with a single keystroke, I tried to show myself to be agreeable. I nodded several times to demonstrate how hard I was listening. I gritted my jaw to indicate that I was accepting a grave responsibility. I murmured, with deep regret, that I hardly ever saw or heard anything, but I would make a special effort. Although I never wanted to have anything to do with the cops, I asked how I should contact him, in the unlikely event that I did learn something.

"Don't worry about that," he said. "I'll contact you."

✦

The cop was correct, of course, about my access to every building in the enclave, residential and commercial, civil and ecclesiastical (though nearly every structure had at least some unofficial lodgers). To reach the equipment, I often had to pass through corridors where people lived or I descended staircases that the migrants had settled with tents or other camping items. Sometimes the equipment panel was installed in small chambers that had been dedicated as closets; other times, in bedroom spaces. In my rounds I became acquainted with the intimate existence of the congested enclave and, by extension, with the American life that had been reconstructed here in all its prosaicness. Kids gazed at the TV as I came through. One of their parents may have been doing laundry in a bucket or making dinner on a Primus stove.

In the basements and subbasements I could feel the press of life above me, a seething human mass that implied more of a metropolis than the district actually was. I sensed it around me too, because tenants occupied other sections of the basement, everything modified to maximize room for living. The buildings, well beyond government inspection, were riddled with cubbyholes, recesses, and imaginatively modified crawlspaces, as well as with baffles and conduits that carried the odors of cooking from one habitation to the other and down to me. These same channels transmitted the sounds of family life, happy and sad, declaratory and plaintive, most of it the fragmented mutters of people, adults and children, who did not require full conversations to make themselves either understood or misunderstood. In one especially grim subbasement I would often hear someone being struck, hurt—a girl or a woman. In every basement, in any building, I encountered the possibility that I would hear someone weeping. Later, in the light, I would look into people's faces, searching for the tracks of recent tears. Two or three times, while I was running a test or switching out a circuit board, I heard the steady beat of lovemaking, a direct message that people were still finding each other and making some kind of sympathetic contact. As I climbed up from the basement, I wondered who among the tenants had just been so fortunate.

Mostly I heard speech I couldn't understand, people referring to something that had been said immediately before my arrival, beyond the range of my hearing, or in response to a visual cue, so it was like lines from an absurdist play. The conversations often had to do, apparently, with shopping for groceries and other necessities, complicated tasks in an impoverished slum.

But in their warrens and in their attic apartments, in their underground nooks and under the quavering fluorescents of colonized cubicle farms, the enclave's residents whispered also of more personal things, about what they wanted in their future lives, ambitions small and large, and also the things that had happened to them in the States, what they heard had happened to other people, and what they themselves had done, either freely or under duress. This history was not something they would have been comfortable sharing on the street or in the market: it ran counter to the spirit of reconciliation that the close-packed neighborhood demanded, that we desperately needed, and, of course, if someone was in earshot, he or she could have disputed their version with a furious counternarrative. Adults told their tales only to their partners and to their children, though the children were only variably receptive. I listened too. Recent history found me through the floorboards, the vents, the dropped ceilings, and the flimsy partitions.

And, unable to shut my ears, I also heard the enclave's most current, most criminal news and gossip. A certain militiaman had arrived from abroad, apparently with money to spend. He was seen being driven around in a new SUV. A previously unknown opioid compound had hit the street. There was a market for it in the western provinces. A network of sex workers had changed hands. I heard someone mention a shipment of unmarked burner phones.

I figured the police already knew about these developments and in any case I didn't know how to reach the detective, and I didn't want to, but the accumulation of intelligence weighed on me. Even without contacting them, I had become an organ of the police, jettisoning the anonymity that was my most secure protection. I more intensely sensed that I was being watched and that my movements through the enclave were being mapped, analyzed, and indelibly recorded, and possibly not only by the police.

Yet I had somehow lulled myself into a denial of this awareness on the morning that the detective next appeared, blocking my way in the littered, muddy alley between a tenement and a slightly more contemporary mid-rise in disrepair. I was surprised. The sun was ascending behind his back, directly in my eyes, casting his face in opaque shadow.

"Ron Patterson?"

The native people thought most Americans looked alike. "Yes, it's me," I said.

"What do you have?"

I told him about the burners, which had been brought in just the previous night. I wasn't sure where they had come from. He didn't show surprise or alarm. He was obviously dissatisfied, so I expanded upon the opioids and the militiaman's arrival, holding back on the prostitutes in the event he pressed further. He watched me carefully as I offered each piece of intelligence.

"That's the best you can do?"

I tried to elaborate, filling in what I knew from my limited eavesdropping and watching: what make the phones were said to be, where the militiaman was said to have flown in from, the color of his SUV. I probably repeated myself several times. I was pretty sure of the opioid's street name at least.

"This is useless," he said. "You know, Ron Patterson, you have no sense of detail, no power of description. Doesn't the militiaman have at least one distinguishing physical feature? Is he short? Is he dark or fair? Does he look like anything? How does he carry himself? Is there an air of mystery about him? Or is he a run-of-the-mill American?"

I wasn't sure why the militiaman's height mattered, but I said I would check.

Before I could tell him about the sex workers, he made a clicking mouth-sound that in this country expressed disgust and he turned back down the alley. He vanished, presumably getting into his car, but I never heard or saw him drive away.

I encountered him again every few weeks. I never knew where this debriefing would take place and I was never aware of his approach. When he appeared, I tried to tell him what I thought he'd be interested in. He made no sign that I had given him anything valuable and I doubted that I did, which was fine with me.

◆

The current national government had come to power promising increased funding for education, even for migrant children, and the enclave's schools, some in repurposed warehouses and factories, represented the state's most significant presence there. The schools offered second-language instruction, as well as the usual mandated curricula, taught by American teachers, who were grateful for their jobs, and natives, who either hated the posting or felt they were carrying out a compassionate mission. Neighborhood school associations were established and some personal contributions to the schools were made by the parents and even, occasionally but generously, by the militias.

I enjoyed doing my school inspections, pushing through the crowds of students in the hallways on my way to the security equipment, wherever it was located. Often I felt myself buoyed on a wave of adolescent glee, the kids totally absorbed by their own jokes, dramas, cliques, and love affairs. These involvements seemed more real to me, more important, than the trivialities that defined adult existence. I recalled my own time at school, so long ago now, but marked by many happy and memorable occasions, save for the last dark year.

The American students all spoke English or Spanish at home, of course. The younger the students, however, the better they spoke the local tongue, and even the high schoolers promiscuously mixed languages. They wouldn't have been well understood beyond the district, but the patois created a kind of generational enclave identity. All the students were exposed to local history and many probably began to see themselves as belonging to the country in which they lived and in which they might live for the rest of their lives. This was especially true of the kids who played the indigenous team sport, a bewildering game without balls or sticks, goalposts or end zones, that nevertheless left them running off the field flushed from their exertions.

During the conflict in the States, much of the nation's public property had been destroyed, damaged, or looted. This included highway signs, mailboxes, bus shelters, subway cars, hospital equipment, the national parks, the zoos, museum collections, and unlaunched spacecraft. Some items showed up abroad, especially where there was a taste for old Americana. The public schools had been no less plundered, mostly to benefit privately run domestic facilities. Some education-related items, however, found their way to the international market and then, with the help of private fundraising and the public-spirited militias, they reached the enclave. In this country native teachers rarely used blackboards, but nearly every classroom in the enclave had one, plus heroically obtained and rigorously conserved blackboard chalk. Looking in as I passed through the hallways, I observed maps, pointers, some chair and desk combinations, English-language encyclopedias kept together with tape and string, alphabet and number charts, faded but legible posters of the periodic table, and lab glassware and equipment. But no classrooms hung American flags. Their display would have been too sentimental or painful or ironic or provocative or open to one misinterpretation or another.

Although the architecture of the schools hardly resembled that of American institutions, and the classrooms were always wrong-size, they seemed like distinctly American places to me. After checking the equipment, I always lingered. I wondered if these children would call themselves Americans as adults, or whether their children would, or whether the native people would ever call them anything but.

✦

The youngsters seemed to get along well enough. Some predictably rejected their parents' competing group identities, their values, and their grievances. They said they didn't care about what had happened in America when they were young or before they were born.

This attitude of disinterest was embraced by the official adult community, at least publicly. With semi-rousing speeches and inclusive social media campaigns, the enclave's non-militia leaders were trying to lift their former countrymen from the abyss into which we had stumbled—almost as if we had made a clumsy mistake, not watching our feet. What had happened was more like a tragic misunderstanding than a dispute that had emerged from vital, tangible differences. Certainly everyone had suffered.

In the former printing plant where I had found sleeping space, all kinds of people lived in close quarters, small children roamed among the decommissioned machines, and they needed peace and security. This was not the place to rehash old arguments, it was said. No one wanted to settle scores, since it was almost an article of faith that the score, back in the States, was pretty much tied up, well into extra innings. We were reminded, too, that both factions had been composed of brave men and women who tried to conduct themselves honorably in a desperate situation not of their own making.

Already late in my fourth decade, I had learned enough about human nature to suppose that this last proposition was probably true. In my travels abroad I had encountered a variety of native partisans arguing a variety of local issues as hotly as we argued ours. I had rarely discerned personal virtue disproportionately allotted to one camp or the other. In any case, because I had left so early during the conflict, missing most of its awfulness, I understood that any political views I did entertain would be considered uninformed.

✦

If I was mostly comfortable with the Americanness of the schools, I still found some dissonance in how the enclave had tried to re-create the American consumer landscape, which had once virtually defined American life. This effort included copies of our famous big-box stores, though they were sited on much smaller lots than the ones they had occupied in the States and the signage wasn't quite right, and more importantly they didn't have anything for sale. They were locked tight and you couldn't see in. Large bouquets of native blooms were occasionally deposited by their doors. Pedestrians hurried by. The structures mutely dominated their streets, but they evidently said something to certain people.

Biking through the enclave, this simulacrum of America, I could never possibly imagine that I had somehow returned home. Yet the experience of living here was essentially American. I was surrounded by Americans and by their hopeless American projects. They brought back to me my childhood, my family, and my friends, all the things I had once taken for granted. I was reminded that any country, like any concept about a place to which you thought you belonged, was a manufactured experience. The American construction was still being attempted here, long after anyone thought it could still make sense.

I came to recognize some passersby, mostly because I had already seen them around the enclave or because they were distinctive American archetypes, members of one demographic or another and very often belonging to a vividly defined microdemographic. It was not unheard of, once every couple of months, to run into an actual individual that you had known in the States. There would be a moment of recognition or perhaps several moments of just fractional recognition.

"Patterson?"

I was kneeling on the sidewalk, locking my bike. I smiled and looked up. The man was standing nearly right above me, which suggested that he had identified me several paces away. This gave him the advantage. I continued to smile, my hand still on the already secured lock, while I delayed rising to my feet.

"It's Dan!" he said, annoyed at my confusion.

I could see how he could be my former high school friend Dan Eisenberg. Sure, why not. As I came to my feet, I clasped his hand, still staring into his face for confirmation. At a loss for what to say, I welcomed him to the enclave.

He said sharply, "I've been here three years now."

He added that he had come to the enclave from another country, where his residency had been brief, implying that he had remained most of the intervening years in the States. I wondered what he had done and what he had witnessed, but these were not things you could ask about. He had been kind of a goof in high school. I didn't see any of that now. He wouldn't have survived if he had remained a goof.

I told him about my own route to the enclave, whose circuitousness was of course nothing unusual, but he nodded politely. I showed him my toolbox and explained my job. He didn't tell me what kind of work he did. I wondered if he was with one of the militias.

We remained on the sidewalk by my bike for about twenty minutes, in casual reminiscence of high school. We mentioned a few classes and swimming in the creek by my fishing spot, staying clear of anything that had a political association, even though our opinions hadn't diverged at the time, to the extent that we had opinions. When we spoke of the people we had known, we didn't speak of what they might have done in the fighting or what they might be doing now, but rather as if they lived only in the high school past, a still-existing past in which they were still challenging each other to drag races on the county road or getting wasted at a camping site in the state park. This didn't mean I didn't want to know.

"How about Ravi?" I finally asked. "Is he still in the States or what?"

Dan looked puzzled.

"Ravi," I repeated. After a few empty moments, I said, "Ravi Satharaman."

The half dozen syllables seemed to bounce around in his head for a while. He put a faraway look in his eyes. "Oh yeah, right," he said at last. "I remember him."

Something was off here, but I said anyway, "Do you know where he is?"

He shrugged. "Nah, how would I know."

"I don't know," I said, matching his shrug. "You were good friends, though. The three of us were."

"You're mistaken," he said evenly. "You're thinking of someone else."

"No, I'm thinking of Ravi," I insisted, pointlessly. "Ravi Satharaman. The three of us. You and him were the guys I launched model rockets with. Remember, we used to go to his house to play video games? And gawk at his two gorgeous sisters? And his mother would feed us, make those big vegetarian dinners for us out of scratch. She was amazing."

He shook his head, almost as if he were trying to shake my words out of his ears.

"Dan!"

He said, "You know, it was a long time ago, and you may think you remember something, some friendship or relationship, some situation or event, but you could be wrong. Memory is so unreliable. You may have constructed a certain past in your head. Maybe it's meaningful, or consoling, or self-validating, or whatever, but it may not be true. That's the way the past is. Anyway, you're wrong about this. I'm telling you, Ron, you're confusing him with another friend. Roberto?"

I kept silent, because I didn't want to argue, but I wondered what happened to the family. It also occurred to me that it was not impossible that he was correct.

After this encounter, the pace of sightings from my town seemed to pick up: the music teacher, a cop, my mother's hairdresser, the dry cleaner, a neighbor who had washed his car every Sunday in his driveway, the cable TV repairman, the minister, the librarian, or at least people who looked like them. For a few years our region of the state had been at the red-hot center of the conflict, so it would not have been surprising that so many of us had left and found our way here. Some of my town's former residents appeared at the corner of my vision or were simply specks in a crowd. We rarely stopped to chat. We might only wave at each other and keep going.

I was getting almost accustomed to these apparitions, but when I recognized yet another familiar person getting out of an SUV across the street, I may have audibly gasped, not that anyone would have noticed. This was someone from my past who had no business being in the American enclave, nor, probably, ostensibly, the correct papers.

I stopped my bike and watched Marlise Larijani cross the strip mall parking lot. She was wearing oversized sunglasses and a fashionable headscarf, as if to defy identification, but in the moment I was sure it was her. The woman didn't pause as she approached two men in suits holding open the door to an all-hours casino.

Remaining on the other sidewalk, I continued to wonder about her papers. I was also aware, in an amused kind of way, that my mind could still be playing tricks on me. It wasn't like I hadn't been thinking of her. Did a day go by in which I *didn't* think of her? Also, it was unlikely for her to be so easily recognized. Many years had passed, hard years for everyone. It didn't occur to me now to follow her into the casino, especially not past the muscle.

I reminded myself of the current geopolitical situation. She would never have been allowed into this country presenting the ruby-red passport that she let me look at our last morning together. She would have needed a passport from somewhere else.

✦

Of course I thought of Marlise every day. Even if it was difficult to recall her face and figure, I never forgot the sweet relief I had discovered in her company. At night now, lying on my back in a hospital cot, the soft snores of other residents in the plant lifting in clouds around me, I often brought myself back to that time and place: the city on the bay, the Corniche, the narrow futon. That succor was like a solid object, indestructible.

Although I had nodding acquaintances among the people with whom I shared the former printing plant, I found it difficult to make friends. Many migrants faced this problem; in the aftermath of the conflict we were isolated and anonymous, diffident about being in society. The enclave was struggling to establish churches and recreational clubs and wherever else we may have met back in the States. Restaurants and bars were too expensive to be frequented by hardly anyone but militia types. I keenly felt my solitude, though I assured myself that it was a simple basic condition of being human. We were mostly alone for most of our lives.

I CONTINUED TO MAKE my rounds, listening in, attentive to what might be of interest to the detective, and I unavoidably found myself taking an interest too. Late one Friday afternoon I was assigned to check the equipment inside an office building that had belonged to a local insurance company before the Americans came to the enclave. I passed through the main entrance and a reception area partially blocked off by plasterboard for living space. I found the service stairway down to a damp, odorous basement. It was strewn with damaged and unsalvageable equipment, including desks, parts of fax machines, and cracked computer monitors. The panel was installed at floor level in an unlit section whose walls were wet with seepage, though what seeped didn't invite examination. I moved some backless swivel chairs and crouched around the glow cast by my flashlight. I was startled then when someone spoke. I thought I had stumbled on yet another human burrow.

No, the voice was coming from above the panel and to the side, behind a wall and above the ceiling. At first I didn't hear what was being said. I didn't move, except to lean in closer to the wall, near the place where the speech was emerging, a small separation between two walls. A man spoke in slow, measured sentences, quietly but urgently, something he was reading or had rehearsed or knew very well. I couldn't follow what he said, but I knew it was about events in the recent American past.

I heard the word "militants." Then I heard the word "checkpoint." Then I heard the name of the town in which I was born and had grown up. The slightly complicated place-name was being enunciated with the clarity of chilled water.

I didn't hear anything further for a few moments. *Home.* The man was evidently moving around the room and what he was saying came and went or it arrived in the basement distorted and muffled. *Home.* I couldn't follow the thread of his story, but I knew that he was speaking of our town and what had happened there. *Home.*

After so many years abroad, America had become for me some kind of abstraction, a bundle of meanings, many of them in opposition to each other. Now the history the man was telling employed proper, skin-prickling nouns, certain roads and streets, shopping centers and malls, the high school, the sports field, the multiplex, and the county administration building. Every one of these names set off a cascade of associations and memories, many of them pleasing. It was pleasingly strange to hear them pronounced while living in a country on the other side of the world.

But I also heard the word "detention." And I thought I may have heard the words "beatings" and "torture." I wasn't sure.

The speech eventually concluded, possibly on a high note, because I heard some applause and cheers. I completed the repairs on the equipment, running late. I left the way I came, up the stairs, into the former reception area. I heard some music and some children at play in the adjoining space. I looked at the outdated building plan I carried with me, trying to determine from where the kindling words had come. It was impossible, the offices had been too carved up and rearranged. In the parking lot I saw boys and young men congregating, smoking cigarettes. There was nobody that I would have recognized from my American past, they were too young. They were about to pile into a van. One of the boys looked at me and I kept my head down and unlocked my bicycle.

That night I tried to piece together what I had heard. I lay in my cot and thought I may have recovered some new words from the man's talk, which I understood now was a lecture or part of a class—a lesson about my hometown. The words slipped and slid around my mind, part memory, part fantasy. These new words were "board," "bodies," "target," "water." In vain I tried to combine and recombine them and find some permutation that could gentle my nerves.

✦

Heard in this context, the sound of my hometown's name provided scant comfort, but shortly after this brush with the past much of my loneliness unexpectedly dissipated. I acquired a dog, one of the many strays that were seen in every section of the enclave, residential and commercial.

On a hazy morning after a service call, crossing between buildings in what had once been a small office park, I caught the attention of a motley gang of eight or nine canines near where my bike was locked. I didn't break my stride (though I reached in my pocket for a locally made canister of pepper spray, its effectiveness dubious). As I approached, the pack's apparent leader barked once and took off in the opposite direction. Only one of the dogs stayed put. It gazed at me. I couldn't identify its breed or assemblage of breeds. I knew nothing about dogs. I stopped and let it study me. I studied it back and smiled, already feeling something. I clapped my hands. "Hey, girl!" I called, and the dog ran toward me in long loping strides, her tongue hanging from her mouth as if it weren't properly attached. She wagged her tail. Neither of us was shy. She came to me and let me ruffle her neck. "Good girl," I said. I named her after the city on the bay.

I had never kept a pet or thought I wanted one, so I was surprised at how much my life would come to revolve around the dog. She had to be fed, of course. She also had to be walked, a task that I discovered I didn't mind and even looked forward to regardless of the weather. This obligation to another living creature, typically assumed by most human beings, was a fresh, belated aspect of my existence. She was disproportionately happy to see me when I returned from work. She bounded across the factory floor, yelping, her tail flicking.

We usually went out to the patches of brown dirt that surrounded the plant and flowed through the spaces between the buildings near it. She inexhaustibly chased a ball, catching it on the fly. I often put her on a leash and we strolled to the shopping street, where other dog owners nodded hello.

People were certainly more sociable when you were accompanied by a pooch. They smiled and might ask its breed, even if it was obviously mixed. Once I had a dog it seemed that everyone in the enclave had a dog, of every size and shape. It would turn out that these sizes and shapes mattered.

Even as I began to allow myself a few stirrings of optimism, I didn't forget what I had heard in the basement. I tried to rehearse what I would tell the detective about it, if anything. I was waiting for our next encounter.

✦

Now that I had been here for some months, I was learning how to read the enclave's social signifiers. Even in flight and exile, even in widespread poverty, even with the imperative to disregard our differences, people maintained distinctions. Clothing and style choices had to be made. Baseball caps could be turned one way or another. Scarfs were loosely or tightly knotted, sneakers were laced straight up or crosswise, sideburns stopped above or below the ears. Everything, even the arm on which you chose to wear your wristwatch, meant something. I myself stayed as inconspicuous as I could manage. I knew how to do this. My survival abroad had always depended on me not signifying anything. I kept the watch in my pocket.

I noticed too that some people discovered a certain import in each other according to the varieties of dogs they owned. They walked their dogs together or waved at each other from across the street. I saw the other dog owners too. If their pets were similar to mine—in either breed, size, or length of hair—they were more likely to acknowledge my presence. I heard people speak of certain breeds with contempt. It was confidently said that certain kinds of dogs were kept by certain kinds of people. You might be able to determine from a dog something about its owner's character or lifestyle or political views, all being close to the same thing.

A few unofficial dog parks were established here and there, another sign of the enclave's deepening Americanization. (The natives didn't keep the animals as pets, but had other uses for them.) While the parks were no more than semi-grassy lots, some of them strewn with construction debris, including cinder blocks and chunks of plaster, they were fenced and the dogs could be unleashed. The animals frisked after balls and each other. Their owners chatted among themselves, mostly about their dogs. The parks were well-used and on some pleasant evenings they assumed an almost party-like atmosphere. I hoped that I might acquire a friend or two in one of these parks.

My own dog was usually well-behaved around other canines, so I hoped she would enjoy the dog park located conveniently close to the former printing factory. I led us through the makeshift gate, which was attached to the fence with a length of twine, and I set her free. She trotted out, tail wagging, and for a moment the other animals stopped what they were doing to watch her, keeping their distance. She went to the center of the lot and spun around a couple of times, waiting. A dog finally came over to sniff and the others followed. This lasted a few moments. Then someone threw a ball and the other dogs left to pursue it. My dog remained, watching, as if she knew the ball was not for her.

I suppose something parallel was happening on the sidelines. I had arrived at the dog park with a smile, but no sympathetic looks came back. One or two looks seemed less than sympathetic.

My dog studied me, though. I threw our old sponge ball, which bounced behind her, and she sprinted after it. She almost had her teeth on the ball when another dog, yapping sharply, grabbed it. The interloper didn't run off; he calmly walked away with the ball. My dog followed him, staying several yards behind. The stranger lay on a sparse swatch of grass and placed the ball between his front paws, an inch off the ball on either side. He snarled when my dog took a step toward it. My dog gave a whimper. I looked across the dog park and I saw the other dog owner watching the exchange intently.

My dog looked back at me, apparently thinking I had a second ball. Like I was made of money. I went over to the other dog. "Hey boy. Let's all play together." Crouching, I carefully reached for the ball. The dog took it, stepped away a few feet, and then again placed it in front of him. I duckwalked closer. He barked, showing his teeth. "C'mon pal," I said. "Don't you want to share?"

The dog owner now towered above us.

"That's my dog."

I stood. "Hi," I said heartily but judged that this wasn't the moment to offer my hand. "Yes, he's a beautiful animal. I was just getting our ball back."

The man made no move to help. He stared, with perhaps military bearing, at his dog and his dog's prize. The dog watched us, reading the situation clearly. The ball remained between his paws. My own pet remained confused. She may have begun wondering whether it had ever been her ball. It looked like her ball, but the other dog seemed utterly confident in his possession.

The man said, "People don't handle other people's dogs, you know."

"I didn't touch him."

He didn't acknowledge the fact. He may have been convinced that I *had* touched him. I walked away, my dog following. I patted her on the flank and she completely forgot about the loss of the ball, but I thought I

would never forget it. I glared at the man. I was determined to remain at least another quarter of an hour. My
dog trotted around the lot, running behind the other
dogs, never actually joining them. I realized, of course,
that there was something wrong with my dog, either she
was of the wrong breed or size for this park, or something else, something I myself couldn't read, or that I
could read but was denying. And maybe I had touched
the other dog. But when I felt enough time had passed, I
clapped my hands and said, more loudly than was necessary, "OK, girl, this has been great. Nice dogs, lovely
people. Let's go home!"

✦

I had never stopped expecting to see Marlise Larijani
again; I had never stopped *demanding* to see her again.
I biked by the casino several times. I looked elsewhere
too. Given the intensity of my desire, it seemed impossible that she wouldn't show up.

Then she *did* show up, except it wasn't the same
woman who had entered the casino. Wheeling a shopping cart out of a poorly provisioned bodega, with
neither the headscarf nor the sunglasses, she closely
resembled Marlise, but she appeared much older than
the woman I had seen. She was older than Marlise
would have been now, less than a decade after we left
the city on the bay. I watched her from afar, identifying

the particular carriage and gait that I thought I remembered from that time. I saw her again crossing the street, appearing even younger than she was when she was the bearer of the ruby-red passport. I biked slowly through the intersection, hoping to hear her call my name.

More women reminded me of Marlise. They were the same height and build, yet they represented every age that a woman could be, from deb to dowager. It was as if a lifetime album of selfies had been scattered around the enclave. I may have seen children who looked like her too.

Yet the glimpse in the parking lot had been fleeting. I still wasn't sure that Marlise had been the woman leaving the SUV and as the weeks passed I became even less confident. I had, of course, experienced this peculiar, person-specific disability elsewhere. I apparently had to accept this frustration, this neuronic misfire, this prosopagnosia, as it was called, as punishment for a long-ago indiscretion or impropriety or misdemeanor. This didn't make it less frustrating.

Now I felt compelled to return to the casino, a low, windowless storefront. I went midday midweek, at the same hour as my first sighting, and I wore my uniform and carried my toolbox. The music was loud, pop hits from a distant land. I passed through the gaming floor, where men and women pulled at machines, flipped cards, and tossed chips in the same desultory manner as they would have performed any other barely remunerative task. They were mostly Americans, in American casual wear. When locals came to the enclave to gamble, they were slumming, but they were usually well-dressed.

My uniform rendered me mostly invisible. I studied the women gamblers and staff leisurely, not sure which of them was the most likely candidate. At the back of the hall I descended stairs to the basement, where I opened the equipment panel, even though it was not due for inspection. Everything was in good working order.

As soon as I returned to the gambling floor, I saw her, the woman I had first thought was Marlise. She wore the same headscarf or a similar headscarf and she was studying a sheet of papers at the end of the bar.

I tried not to show my excitement. I approached in measured steps, giving her time to raise her head. She didn't.

I stopped and said, "Hey."

Now she looked up. Distracted by the figures on the page, she didn't seem to really see me. She didn't say anything.

"I just inspected the equipment," I said. "It's working optimally."

"All right."

"I wanted to make sure you knew."

She didn't respond for a moment. Our company and its inspectors weren't obliged to report the status of the equipment to residents or commercial tenants. We rarely had official interaction with them at all.

"Thank you," she eventually murmured.

"You're welcome," I said. Then I grinned. "I'm Ron Patterson!"

These words never grazed her consciousness. There was no smile or grimace or movement in her eyebrows or even a quick study of the speaker's face. She didn't offer the merest artifact of recognition.

"OK," she said. "Thanks again."

✦

Elsewhere, at least, I was starting to become half-familiar to the other Americans, either for my slick company uniform and my jaunty cap, or from an earlier existence without uniform and cap. A head would turn perhaps a quarter of an inch, eyes would widen, and the glimpsed image of my face would laboriously swim through a deep-green sun-shadowed consciousness toward what might be a name. But sometimes the name was right there.

"Ron-a-rino."

I slowed and stopped my bike at the curb by an automotive body shop. Only one of my high school friends had ever called me Ron-a-rino, and he had done so regularly in a playful kind of way, but I couldn't remember who it had been. This man, with some oily rags in his hands, gazed at me now with a fixed stare, not playfully. His gibe had been flat and dispassionate. A couple of guys in the garage looked up. The shop was apparently thriving, with two cars lifted on the racks and a few others in the driveway outside.

The man said, "You don't recognize me?"

I smiled, trying to be friendly. "I'm sorry. It's been so many years."

He declared, "You've just come here."

The fellows in the shop had paused in their work, to observe our exchange. Some stood back from their equipment, crossed their arms, and studied me. They waited for my response.

"Yeah, a few months ago. I love it," I said. This was at least an exaggeration. "How are you doing? What are you up to?"

The man didn't answer, so I told him for whom I was working and what I did, just to make conversation.

"Ron. A. Ri. No," he said.

"Yeah, it's me. Well, I'm on the clock. See you around."

"Wait."

I was still on my bike, smiling uneasily. He reached into the pocket of his windbreaker and produced a chewed-up sponge ball.

"Wow," I said. "Thank you."

"You have some problem at the dog park?" he asked. I thought I heard a challenge.

"Not really," I said. "Some dog took the ball away."

"Nobody took your ball."

"It was no big deal," I said. "Dogs see balls and they take them."

He shook his head. "Your dog left the ball in the dirt. Another dog picked it up after you left."

I reminded myself what I had seen with my own eyes. I kept it in front of me. The effort, though, produced an almost physical pain, as it always did. It ran like a hot wire from the optic nerve to the seat of consciousness. Very likely the man saw my pain but didn't care. The mechanics were auditing this conversation from the garage.

The man asked what kind of dog I had. I described her accurately but prudently, without classifying her by breed or by mixture of breeds and without naming those attributes that might have identified her kind. I said she was friendly.

"Maybe you should go to another dog park."

"That's the one near where I live." To soften the note of defiance, I added, "Or maybe get a new dog."

"Yeah."

"I'm not trying to make trouble," I said, sounding more plaintive than I intended. "I didn't mean to offend anyone."

"Listen to me, Ron."

His manner changed now. He told me that I might have known his brother, David, who was several years older than us. He had become a doctor. He was driving back late at night from the county hospital. He worked in intensive care. Some men were setting up a roadblock. They had just begun, putting guys in position, unloading the sand barrels. His brother was too smart to run a roadblock. He simply never saw it or he didn't understand that they were establishing a roadblock. So David kept driving and one of the men fired into the car. It was so stupid, so pointless, that even the guys knew it. They brought him back to the hospital, very apologetically, but he was already dead.

"I'm sorry," I said, struggling to recall anyone whose older brother had attended medical school. Only one friend, Audrey, had a brother named David, and he hadn't been medical school material. "I know bad things happened."

"And you're going to ask me which side, right? Who did it? Do I know the gunmen? Sure I do. You may have known them too, from high school or the church. One of them's here. When I see him he looks away. I also look away. But both sides had checkpoints. Both sides were sloppy with their gun use. I can't do anything about what happened on the road that night. My wife's pregnant. I'm only thinking about the child now, what kind of life he or she's going to have here. Every incident, every microaggression, every trigger is a danger to this child and to other children. You understand that, right?"

I understood. I was aware too that this man, whose name I still couldn't excavate, had been waiting for me. He had been told I would be passing this shop around a certain time. Someone had given him the sponge-ball and told him to be there.

At the printing plant I returned the ball to my dog and she only sniffed at it. I picked it up myself. Did it have the wrong scent now, the other dog's? My dog had forgotten the ball. Her history with it had simply slipped from her dog-brain. As I studied the ball, I wondered if there was some confusion about the object itself, if indeed this was the same ball we had brought to the dog park. It may have been the wrong size or color or sponge consistency, I thought. The bite marks didn't seem correct either, more likely belonging to a bigger dog or a smaller one. No, a mistake could have been made. This may not have been hers at all.

✦

Yes, I understood. Most people were trying to think about the future they would make in this strange new country. The tense relative peace among us was like the aftermath of a drenching rain, the air still fogged with humidity, the humidity still capable of being regathered, yet the streets were drying. Community leaders announced steps toward reconciling the diverse Americans who had found safety here. I myself could see, in the few months since I had arrived, material improvements in the district, mostly cafés and nail salons opening for business.

A local English-language media was beginning to constitute itself, distinctly and self-consciously less partisan than it had become in the States. Several programs presented "exposés," some quite disturbing, about how our countrymen had been manipulated—by social media, by cable news, by broadcast news, by newspapers, by internet memes, and also by movies and television shows, even sitcoms, and also by novels, poems, pop songs, and commercial advertising.

We discovered that the conflict, as painful and tragic as it had been, was really a contest between *texts*, each telling the history of our country plausibly and compellingly and neither necessarily built on untruths. Opposing narratives, we learned, could easily be constructed from the same actual occurrences and objective facts. Additional information (a recent provocation, a piece of demographic data, a politician's accidental candor) could be valued by one side and discounted by the other, even though both could agree that the reporting was technically correct. It was only a matter of storytelling.

I mostly accepted the history of the conflict as it was now being presented in the enclave. There were certainly many elements—situations and atrocities, paragons of fortitude and marvels of human sympathy—with which I wasn't familiar. I knew from having lived in other foreign places, however, that some of this storytelling couldn't be true or that at least it wasn't being entirely rightly told. I had seen reports from America in the foreign media, which had biases and political obligations of their own, but their distortions hadn't always slanted along the same partisan lines as ours. So you could learn something.

And I knew that the contest *hadn't* been equal, whatever personal virtues adhered to individual partisans. Both sides had *not* suffered equally. A roughly equal number of atrocities was *not* committed by both sides. Both sides had *not* contributed equally to the misunderstanding, which was really *not* a failure of communication but was rather a single side's self-interested distortion of American history and its willful blindness to contemporary wrongdoing.

Of course, I brought my own history and prejudices to the argument.

I additionally recognized that it was predictable for me to believe that the side that had suffered more and sinned less was the one with which I had once been loosely affiliated. It was maddening.

At every place in the enclave we lay in our cots, our bunks, and our beds wondering, our eyes jolted open, how those in the neighboring sleeping spaces could believe what they believed. It was so contrary to established historical fact, or so contrary to science or long-standing moral values, obvious stuff, that they may have just as well been disputing simple arithmetical equations. We tried to see it their way and the effort left us on the brink of derangement. Objective reality slipped from our grasp, leaving us unable to trust our senses or our ability to reason. They were lying. They thought we were lying. We couldn't prove we weren't. Which didn't prove that at least one of us *wasn't* lying.

We could hardly keep still.

✦

Within two weeks the equipment at the former insurance office transmitted some urgent error messages, indicating a more complicated problem. I returned to the building, but now, as I switched out the board and ran some tests, all I heard above my head was the shallow drip of unattended plumbing.

My supervisor reported that the latest repair was a success and the new panel was functioning normally, but I was determined to return to the building. I came the following Friday afternoon, the same time of day as my first visit, and now I observed more young men in the parking lot. They noticed me too. I looked away, swinging my toolbox. A few other men were headed for an entrance in the back of the building. I again went through the main entrance and down to the basement.

I opened the panel, conscientiously checking the equipment. Everything worked. I heard the scuffling of chairs above me. In a moment the lecture began. The speaker was some kind of teacher, I thought, in a class that was not incorporated into any official curriculum. The class couldn't have been, not with that language.

"Storage cages," I heard. Also the name of my town, again thrillingly. Also "interrogation." Also "snipers." The word "target" came up again, but it wasn't employed in a way that made immediate sense. It was repeated a few times, an element of a story that was unfolding slowly, with diversions and false starts. The class interrupted to ask questions, but I couldn't hear the questions. The teacher's lesson reasserted itself.

I leaned toward the crack in the wall, into the flow of language, the flow of history, aware that I wouldn't want to be found out, either by my supervisor or by the guys on whom I was eavesdropping. They had looked like tough guys. A continuous and complete story continued to elude me, but certain phrases, introduced in the course of the broken narrative, repeated themselves: "they hate us," "what they've done to us," "it's justice," "it's time," "protecting ourselves," "our children," "our children," and "our children." Also, there was an element of prediction. The increasingly strident speaker invoked the near future: the following night, in fact. As Saturday slid into Sunday, men would be moved into position. I also came to understand that the initial letter of the word whose meaning I hadn't been sure about was capitalized.

An hour must have passed. I had stayed too late and would have to conduct the remainder of my assigned inspections later that evening. But in that hour, in the stink of the basement, my face pressed against the filth, the words, the episodes, the accidents, the

abominations, and the calamities came at me in a fero-
cious roar. The men were again receiving the history of
events that had brought them to this place. And then
the roar stopped and I heard another word, or rather it
was the name of a human being, a character in the story
being told. Delicately, so that his listeners would not
record the name incorrectly, if they were taking notes,
the instructor or activist or agitator or warlord had
spoken the vowels and consonants that composed the
identity of a despised person who was once, in America,
very slightly, very distantly familiar to me.

Or perhaps not, I thought later, when I was com-
pleting my rounds, undressing for bed, and then putting
myself to sleep. I recognized that in the basement the
words being spoken had reached me imperfectly, like so
much of America's garbled history. These could have
been other words, perhaps not the name of a person,
or maybe they were the name of some other person. I
wasn't sure. I knew that I had a tendency to be confused.
I had been wrong about many things before. I knew, too,
that Amanda Keller had been on my mind, making me
more susceptible to aural hallucination.

✦

I thought now for sure the detective would appear and he
did, early the next morning, before I left for work, while
I was walking my dog in a semi-secluded wooded area

behind the printing plant. He stood off the path, partly obscured by the leafy trees. He smoked a cigarette, or rather this country's approximation of a cigarette.

"There's going to be violence," I said. "One of the militias is planning an attack."

"Violence," he repeated, struggling to recall the word's meaning in English.

I asked him if he had noticed the shuttered miniature big-box stores around the enclave. They weren't really places of business, I explained. They were more like shrines, reflecting recent American events. I tried to explain these events. I told him that when the national economy had collapsed, all the American retail chain companies went bankrupt. Thousands of their strategically located warehouse-size stores were abandoned. I wasn't sure he followed me, so I attempted to repeat myself in the local language.

"No, no," he said, exhaling a cloud of smoke that further obscured his native features. "Speak English. I can understand. My father was from Mumbai."

Nothing about him looked Indian, but I went on in English. I told him that across the country these buildings had been seized by militias, including those controlled by the contending national, state, and local authorities. Opposition fighters had to be held, sympathizers had to be interrogated, potential sympathizers had to be interrogated, troublemakers had to be sequestered, some people had to be punished, and more people had to be interrogated. These gigantic, window-less, open-plan stores were perfectly suitable. Because of America's severe polarization, no one was surprised when one side became identified with one former chain retailer, while its principal adversaries assumed control of the stores that had belonged to its main competitor and other militias took control of lesser competitors.

"What a fucked-out country," he muttered, not quite conforming to standard usage.

It was, I agreed. That was why I was grateful to be allowed to live in his country, I added, in all sincerity. All the migrants were grateful, I said, but there were still some partisans, some rivalries, some bones left unpicked, and some bad memories. I tried to explain how these memories were being kept alive. Some people felt they needed to show respect for history. Some people needed justice. They also needed to remind their former opponents that they were here. This was done with signs and symbols obscure and covert. Thus each side had erected somewhere in the enclave a model of the big-box store that was associated with its people's struggle. Weren't the police aware? Now one of the structures, the miniature Target, was about to be attacked. The militia that had occupied the competitor's stores was planning something. I wasn't sure of the hour.

The detective grimaced and shook his head at the whole American nonsense. I still wasn't sure how much he understood.

"People live on that street," I said. "The tenements are packed. And the other side's going to want revenge."

He withdrew into the woods. I returned my dog to the factory, filled her water bowl in the men's room, and brought her to our little space behind a left-behind one-ton paper roll. I went off on my rounds as I always did, as if the encounter had never happened.

That night was Saturday night, which even for Americans in reduced circumstances maintained an aura of occasion. The urge to go out was still there. Couples strolled hand in hand. Music thumped from inside the casinos, their pavements flooded with light that seemed to etch in stone the shadows of the sex workers stationed on the corners. As I walked my dog that night, I thought the district was a little noisier and more animated than usual, yet there was also less traffic, on the streets and on the sidewalks, but this could have been something I imagined.

I went back to my cot in the factory and couldn't sleep, no matter how many comforting images I summoned to my bedside. It was unclear whether anyone was sleeping around me. I could hardly hear anyone breathe, much less snore. How could anyone sleep beneath the machinelike humming drone that now permeated the enclave?

Rarely did I leave the factory past midnight. The streets could be unsafe. Now I couldn't stop myself from heading toward the boulevard where the Target memorial was located. Others seemed to feel the pull too, walking ahead of me and behind. Some murmured, telling themselves stories about our shared past.

I never reached the Target. At the corner of the block I stopped among a crowd of bystanders. They were watching as about a dozen men in distinctive leather coats milled around the building. The men were waiting. The memorial continued to stand, defiant and vulnerable. The buildings alongside the building were being evacuated, at least, but the tenants were angry. There was some shoving. The men were stronger and they had sticks.

The SUV that shortly screeched to a stop at the curb discharged more people than I thought it could have possibly contained, including a man of uncommon height. He slowly unfolded himself from the vehicle. I might have recognized some of the individuals from the parking lot outside the former insurance company building where they had received their assignments. They carried large green cans of kerosene; oddly, kerosene cans were green in this country. The men who were waiting cleared the way. Even before the last passenger debouched, the first put down a line of rags and newspapers on the ground where the building met the sidewalk. Another man began emptying the can. The tall man watched. The air sweetened sharply. Those of us on the corner took a few steps back.

We were now roughly pushed aside by the arrival of several men issuing threats. One shouted, "You want a war? You have a war!" A few carried baseball bats and there were other things, I saw, that could also be used as weapons. They rushed forward.

Once the melee began, it was hard to follow, and it went on for some time, no one having guns, which were strictly regulated in this country. Some of the guys, however, had knives and chains and brass knuckles. Punches were thrown. I saw a bat connect once or twice, sickeningly. Men went down. More fighters showed up for both sides, in matching white SUVs. The attackers managed to get a fire lit. The Target defenders initially put it out with a household fire extinguisher. Everyone saw that it would be inadequate.

Then: *whoosh!* Even the attackers were surprised. They fell back, shouting, and the crowd gasped almost in carnival pleasure. In a few moments the structure was obscured by a sheet of flame.

The defenders gave up protecting the building. The attackers drove away and the fire captured the adjacent structures. The sleepy, confused children who had occupied the tenements watched the fire from across the street with their parents, some of the smaller kids perhaps not aware of its consequences.

The adults in the crowd were wide-eyed and speechless, the diversity of shades in the American face diminished to slightly varying, rippling tints of orange that reflected the fire. But the precise moment-to-moment image of the blaze, every flicker and flash, could be seen on our eyes' convex, moist outside surfaces. A snap, a crackle, a pop: we wondered what artifact had just lost its external form within the bowl of the conflagration. We waited for the familiar cries of approaching sirens. There were none. We were entirely on our own, as we had been for some time. The city's distant skyline continued to glitter under the cold, blind stars. The fire would have to extinguish itself.

✦

The site smoldered for another week while a twenty-four-hour militia guard surrounded the other big-box memorial, to protect it from retaliation. Dozens of families who had lived adjacent to the Target dispersed across the district, where housing was still haphazard and scarce. They had lost everything they owned. Their daily routines were disrupted. The new living arrangements sundered whatever bonds had formed between neighbors, including their friendships and their communal arrangements. The enclave's media, however, never reported the attack. It would have been too much of an incitement, even if the population was universally aware of what happened.

The national government eventually took notice of the destruction and early one morning, without

announcement, a convoy of trucks, backhoes, and bull-
dozers entered the enclave, accompanied by police cars
with flashing lights. The native contractors worked
quickly. They removed what was left of the Target and
the surrounding buildings: burnt wood and drywall,
tangles of rebar, some unusable household items (the
usable items had been scavenged). The foundations
were filled in, leaving a smooth dirt lot half a block wide
and a full block deep. The convoy left the district at
nightfall, led again by the police. When the equipment
returned the following morning, the crew demolished
the still-standing memorial to the fighters affiliated with
the other big-box store, scattering its guards, the same
men who had torched the Target.

I watched the cops from hidden vantage points around
the cleanup sites, but I didn't recognize my detective.

Weeks later no one had claimed the sizable, conveniently located empty lots, neither to pitch a tent nor raise
a lean-to nor put up some other unofficial residential or
commercial structure, as was done in nearly every other
available vacant place in the enclave. When I biked past
either site, I noticed that pedestrians were using the sidewalks only on the opposite sides of the streets. They gazed
straight ahead. No one crossed the former Target lot to get
to the next block, as if the building were still there.

But it *wasn't* there. I began to be annoyed at the
pretenses that governed our lives in the enclave. My
unease may have originated, ironically enough, with

my *ease* here, a deepening sense that this place, populated by Americans and furnished with half-American
or pseudo-American artifacts, was in fact my home,
my America, perhaps the only territory in the world
where I could legally and safely live. If this was to be
my home, then, I had a right to be dissatisfied with several other features of the place too: the violence, the
squalor, the low wages, the militias, the detective, my
living conditions. Not that I intended to do anything
about them.

On a Sunday afternoon when I would attract some
unwelcome, unfortunate attention, I didn't set out on
my dog-walking route with any expectations. We left the
factory, passed through the woods, eventually reached
the district's main commercial area, and then went
down one side street or another. I thought I was letting the creature at the other end of the leash direct me,
according to her dog-whims. But perhaps she too was
wondering about the empty lot at the former Target site.

I was aware of the residual odors of the fire half a
block away and also, as we approached, that we were
alone on the sidewalk. Then we were in front of the lot.
My dog pulled on the leash. I pulled back. She whim-
pered. Stepping onto the pristine lot, I almost expected
quicksand. No, the ground held, as firm as any terrain
my adult self had ever walked on. I took another step and
turned to see who else was around. No one. I went a few
more yards, sensing myself unaccountably free and also

reckless in a way that I hadn't been reckless for years. I realized now how much I had missed this feeling.

I unleashed the dog. She sped off across the lot, kicking up small grains of dirt. She too was declaring her freedom. I threw her a high pop fly. It was a new ball, just acquired. She let it fall and then leaped to catch it at the top of its first bounce.

The lot was featureless, limited left and right by the tenements that had been spared by the fire. These were low buildings, leaving plenty of mottled sky above us. There were few places in the enclave that owned so much sky. At the far end of the lot, the next street of homes, stores, and car traffic conducted its regular business.

We played. I threw the ball further and the dog became even more adventurous in going for it, her body airborne for seconds at a time. She returned the ball and dropped it at my feet, squealing in self-congratulation. She saw through my head fakes and pretend throws, waiting patiently, tongue out, for the actual launch and I was increasingly aware of our aloneness. We had come to the center of the vacant lot, which now seemed immense. Cars were slowing as they passed.

The abandon of a few minutes earlier now felt like a fatuity of youth. I threw the ball a few more times. It was evident that drivers on the streets at both ends of the lot found us interesting. I waved the leash and clapped my hands. "OK girl, let's call it a day!"

The dog didn't respond. She decided to poop, which

I suppose she would have argued was the whole rationale for the walk. She took her time. I went over to where she squatted, a tremor in her haunches.

"C'mon." I shook the leash, but she paid no attention, lost in a poop-trance. I knew that she was very committed to her poops. I'd have to wait. It was coming out in a single, smooth, deep-black, deep-bowel extrusion. Even in the warmth of the day, a shimmering mist ascended from the enlarging pile. The odor was distinctly her own, sour and earthy, refracting the kitchen scraps I fed her. I looked away, first at some clouds low on the horizon and then behind me, where a white SUV was slowly rolling by. It stopped. I returned to the poop as if it were the most fascinating thing in the world.

The pile was getting even larger, more poop than I had ever seen her evacuate, and she showed no sign of strain or fatigue and no sign of stopping. Nor had there been any indication of intestinal discomfort beforehand: no canine whining or farting. She had pooped normally that morning outside the printing plant. She was pooping normally now, but to a prodigious extent. I could tell without looking back that the SUV remained at the curb. An identical white SUV mirrored it at the other end of the lot. I wished that I had at least brought a plastic bag.

I waved the leash in the dog's face. I wondered where the poop was coming from. Its mass seemed to approach the total weight of the dog. Where had she stored it? How long had it been accumulating? The dump, with its steeples and its turrets, its well-defined stories and wings, and its apparently purposeful recesses and protrusions, looked almost like a piece of architecture. I gazed at it, trying to extract meaning. How would the dog behave after she rid herself of this excess matter? Would there be a personality change? I studied the poop's clumps, fanciful whirls, and little sparkly bits of undigested food. Perhaps the shit was something else, not a building, but rather a multitiered, multiwalled, messily stacked-up reverie of human history.

When she was at last finished, the dog stepped away and obediently nudged her head against the leash. The vehicles had left. The pile of course remained, the only thing in the lot, still faintly fuming.

✦

Even with the SUVs gone, even with me returning to my living space in the factory, even with me performing my regular rounds in the enclave, even with me not going back to the empty lot, I became aware that I was being observed with new interest, or at least that I had gained a certain notability or significance. This seemed to have happened immediately, starting the evening we came back and the considerably reduced dog and I passed the defunct web-offset machines on the way to our space, her nail-clicks echoing off the cement floor. The other residents stopped for a moment and watched. They hadn't watched before. I saw looks in the street and when I entered buildings to inspect equipment. Sometimes I thought the looks were suspicious or slightly antagonistic, sometimes they were warm, and once I received a furtive glance that suggested fear. Despite having plenty of room to pass, a car followed me on my bike for half a minute, before zooming off.

After all these years abroad I thought I knew how to be unremarkable, how to be anonymous. Speak softly. Be indifferent to public rudeness. Wear off-brand jeans, off-brand shoes, and wrinkle-resistant button-downs. Hold yourself small. Cross at the light, unless, as was the case in a few cities in which I had lived, no one did. Literally keep your head down. I had begun to relax my guard in this country's American district—and the venture into the empty lot broke every personal rule— but now I resumed the manners that had kept me safe. I became accustomed to the extra attention, which in the next few weeks I thought had diminished.

This turned out not to be the case.

I was in a small back room in the garage of a former vehicle depot, fiddling with a circuit board that tested normally outside the unit but sent error messages when it was reinstalled. Now I was checking the contacts. The garage was cool and dimly lit and the air tasted of machines, a pleasing odor that suggested power and utility. I was deeply immersed in my task, so the sound of an unlocked door opening behind me didn't register.

People were always moving about these buildings any-way. I rarely took notice. Shortly, though, I was aware that someone had joined me.

I thought it was the detective, at last. I hadn't seen him since the morning I had given him the only useful information I ever had.

"All right," I said lightly. "One minute."

A man said, "How ya doin'?"

I turned from the panel. The man was a stranger, but obviously an American.

"Good," I said. "But this unit could be shot. I may have to replace it. Just going to run a few more tests."

"Cool."

Two other men entered the cramped alcove. They sported similar haircuts and wore leather jackets in the same style, possibly coincidentally or possibly not. They were relaxed and open-faced. I did notice, however, that they more or less occupied the space between me and the door to the room.

The first guy came toward me, his arm extended. I tensed. "Buster Williams!" he nearly shouted. He grabbed my right hand.

I introduced myself.

He repeated my name as if he were savoring it. "Ron Patterson," he exclaimed. He pumped my arm and squeezed my right bicep. He added, "You're the man. You're the fucking man."

I smiled, not trying to hide my confusion.

He asked me where I was from. I told him the name of my company and that I lived in the former printing plant.

"You dickwad. I mean in America."

I knew, of course, what he meant. I was stalling. Finally, I told him the name of my state. He was interested, so I was obliged to tell him the name of the town, which I knew would signify some recent American history, one way or another. He showed more interest. He said he was from the same county, but from a town two towns over. His town had one of those generic names that appeared on the map of nearly every state. Now he looked at me warily.

"Small world," I said. "Hey, I'm going to be done in five minutes. We can catch up outside."

"No, let's talk here. But if you want to finish up, go ahead. I can hold the flashlight for you."

I preferred not to have other people around me while I worked. I quickly adjusted the contacts and reinserted the board. It seemed OK now. I could return if the unit malfunctioned again.

The corner of the damp, low-ceiling room, where we were crammed between the door and the unit, was an awkward place to talk, but Buster didn't mind. The other men showed no discomfort either.

He observed, "Lots of bad shit went down in your town."

I conceded that it had, but I had missed most of it. I had left so early, I said. Buster wanted to know which year, and when I told him, he wanted to know which month. Something had happened nearly every day of that year—another incident, another development—and every month was heavy with import.

"So, like, what did you think of it?"

What *did* I think of it? I had thought of it a lot, of course. The bad shit had come so fast, fresh news every hour of the week, that you were always receiving another piece of information or an idea or a lesson that you would have to fit into your understanding of things. But my principal thought then, or brooding worry, was that I would be recruited by one side or the other. Given certain minor affinities, there was only a single side that would have been likely to. I was mostly interested in getting out of the country while I could.

I now told Buster that the conflict had been a tragedy, hoping the catch in my throat suggested fiercely repressed deep feeling. I added that there was so much history behind what had happened, some of it very complicated. I was hardly an expert. Good, patriotic people simply had contrasting opinions. But I still believed in American values. I still believed in the country.

"Right," he said slowly.

He studied me, his smile fading as his expression turned contemplative. The guys with him picked up on the change in mood, but their faces couldn't match his friendly thoughtfulness. The attitude they adopted was something else. I continued to smile,

innocently I hoped. I *was* innocent. I believed everything I said, more or less. Not knowing which side
he had been on, I couldn't be sure exactly which
response was called for.

He said what a great place the former printing plant
was, kind of neat in an urbanist, postindustrial way, I
must enjoy living there. He had seen me on my bike. He
said biking was terrific exercise, I looked totally ripped.
He asked me which was my favorite casino and when I
told him I hadn't been to any, he laughed. He gave me a
card. He winked and told me I'd be comped.

"So," he said casually, "what's up with the dog?"

"She's great. What do you mean?"

"No, what does *she* mean?"

"My dog? She's a dog. She means nothing."

"Mutts can be anything, huh," he said. "I've heard
that before. Like a mixed breed is some kind of compro-
mise, some kind of negotiated settlement—a consensus
dog, right? Interesting."

He was quiet for a moment, taking pains to assem-
ble his thoughts. His men waited intently, ready to listen to every word. I saw that one of them had a stick
under his belt.

"Look, Ron," he said at last. "Everything has a goddamn meaning. We live in a world of fucking signs and
symbols, all of it man-made. Human beings fight over
this shit even more than we fight over money, which
itself is a symbol of the most fucking trivial kind. It's

these signs and symbols that make history, that make the *telling* of history useful."

"If it is useful," I said.

The guys shifted, as if ready to push back on any foray into nihilism.

He said, "Take, for an example, an empty lot. It's technically a public space, am I right? It's a fucking blank page. It's almost begging to be written on. It's almost begging for meaning—unless it already has meaning, because nothing is truly vacant. Right? So if you're going to *add* to its meaning, people are going to want to know your underlying message—your subtext, if you will. How you think about things." He paused, to see if I was following him. Unfortunately, I was. He went on: "If you simply walk through the lot, staring at your feet or the sky, you're imparting one meaning. You've designated the park as a space for relaxation, for reflection, for looking at the fucking sky. If you walk your *dog* there, you're endowing it with another use. If you allow your dog to poop there, that's, for Chrissakes, imparting a meaning too, which some people may find either challenging or celebratory, depending on how they understand it. So there's going to be interest in understanding your meaning, in *reading* the text you've composed on the unblemished surface of the empty lot, explicit and implicit. People will want to know its intent."

We were about to be interrupted. Footsteps were heard outside the room, chuffing across the shed's cement floor.

Buster stopped to listen, as if to a distant air. We could tell the tread belonged to a woman. The four of us turned.

The woman materialized in the doorway. She was an unfamiliar middle-aged American who wore a two-piece suit whose style might have once been called business casual. These two words were now faintly oxymoronic, at least in the gangster-ridden enclave, and the outfit might have signaled something entirely different. She scowled. The younger men stepped out of her way.

"Buster, stop it!"

"We're having a conversation."

She barely glanced in my direction.

"Leave him alone. He just came here. Not everyone cares about semiotic theory like you do."

Buster stared at me for a moment, to indicate that the discussion wasn't finished, but he was evidently surprised. Something else was working in his face too, something at least like annoyance. He looked away not to show it. His embarrassed companions also found elements of the basement alcove to study.

She approached, unsmiling. "Hello, Ron. We were in eleventh-grade physics together. Mr. Strauss? I sat behind you, in the back of the class. Nikisha Jones." She locked eyes with me, her face hard. "Buster's my husband."

"That was a great class," I said. "Those experiments."

"You know each other?" Buster said, a question directed at the woman. He was still angry. I also detected the tautening of his vigilance.

"Not really," I said. I hoped I didn't sound too emphatic about it. "It was a long time ago and a really big school."

This was true. I had hardly known Nikisha Jones. Once on a ninth-grade field trip we rode the bus together and managed a decently friendly boy-girl conversation. After that, for another year at least, we acknowledged each other with a smile or a nod when we passed in the hall. Then we were separated by the usual transformations of adolescence and the additional divisions that marked our high school years, and we stopped showing that we recognized each other. But Nikisha never looked anything like this woman. Also, Nikisha and I were never in the same physics class nor any other.

"It was a huge school," she confirmed. "We were in that one class though."

"I learned a lot," I said. And then I added, trying to be offhand about it, "I remember you. I've thought of you more than once over the years."

She gave no indication that she had thought of me.

Buster said, "I need to find out about the dog."

"No you don't," she told him. "Let the man finish his job."

"I had just a few questions. You know, about certain denotations and connotations."

"C'mon, Buster."

With Nikisha's head turned, Buster gazed at me as if to remember what I looked like, or to remind me that he knew what I looked like. The men looked at me too. I tried to smile. They filed from the room, Nikisha behind them.

"Hey," I said quietly to the back of her head. "Hey. Did we know each other somewhere else?"

The men had retreated, their boots clattering. They hadn't heard me speak.

I pressed the question in a whisper. "How long have you been here? Where have you lived?"

She turned to face me, fury in her eyes, her jaw set.

"You don't ask people those kinds of questions," she said, her voice low but penetrating. "Where we went. Who we knew. How we survived."

One of the men at the outer door to the garage had stopped, probably Buster. He was waiting for Nikisha to come. We heard him take one step back. She remained where she was, inches from my face, implacable. Some other thought, a fresh shadowy image, sparked across my brain stem. It came from that class in physics, but I couldn't see what it was, though I did remember now that Strauss had given me only a B-plus for the year.

"I once knew somebody who reminded me of you. A long time ago."

"Just watch what you do, Ron. People here are in pain and they're pissed off. After the fire, everyone's on edge. Something's going to happen, I don't know what. Stay away. Don't get yourself hurt."

I let her exit and I gave Buster and the guys plenty of

time to leave the parking lot. *Buster Williams*: the name dropped again into the well of memory and this time, after a while, I may have heard a distant splash.

I didn't open the unit again. Instead I stood there and contemplated the corner of the garage in which I found myself—the single bare bulb overhead hanging from a loose wire, the grit-coated floor, the sweet machine odor, the underlying notes of leaking chemicals—and considered the irresistible currents of world events in which we simply treaded water, really no more than bobbing, sinking flotsam.

The business card was still in my hand. I checked the address. It was not the casino where I had been.

✦

The detective finally showed the next day, just as I was about to leave a tottering brick tenement jammed with families. He walked me back into the building, down into the shadows of the basement, and then into one of the basement's corners. He seemed even bulkier than before. He could have crushed me like one of those indigenous cockroaches.

"What do you have?"

I said, "I had something last time. Look what happened!"

This was a sharper tone than I was accustomed to using with foreign officials, especially those in law enforcement. The detective didn't respond, perhaps not understanding my rebuke or the tone in which it was delivered. I would have to restrain myself. I now related more coolly how I had gone for a walk with my dog across the former Target site and the dog had pooped there. It was an inadvertent thing, I said. I told him then that this was followed by a harmless encounter with some guys. I was careful not to identify the guys. I was very vague about my interview with them.

"What's inadvertent?"

I told him that it meant unintentional or negligent and then, when he showed no comprehension, I went through a virtual thesaurus of synonyms: careless, thoughtless, etc. The further I traveled down the list, the less persuasive I sounded.

"But why did you let your dog poop there?"

He didn't understand my shrug. He questioned me further about my visitors, his irritation rising. What were their names? Did I know with which side they were associated? What did they want?

"It was only a chat," I insisted. "We talked about text, subtext, and narrative. You know, typical American things."

He shook his head. He said he couldn't understand American things. He couldn't understand how Americans thought or what they hoped for, about what they dreamed or about what they wept, what they loved or about what they were fighting. For him the district was a maze and every turn led to a dead end. There was no tofu, as far as he was concerned. (Mice in this country preferred tofu.) I offered that in fact the district wasn't so bad. He said it was predictable for an American to think so. I said that not every predictable belief was incorrect.

"They didn't tell you their names? How many of them were there?"

I told him three: three men.

"Three men," he repeated.

"That's right," I confirmed,   ·

The lie brought fierce heat to my face, but I wasn't sure if a blush was a tell that a native-born person could observe.

The detective fixed a stare on me for a while. I saw pain in his eyes and I felt some sympathy for him before I remembered that he was a cop.

He said finally, "There's no point talking to you."

"I agree."

He made a peculiar native grimace, what passed for a scowl.

"Listen, Ron Patterson. Something's going on. I need to know what it is. If you're lying, God damn you . . . keep your eyes out for these guys, figure out who they are, what they want, what they're going to do." He added, "I'm not the only one who wants to know."

✦

I still needed to walk the dog and I found another park, less handily located, where after a few afternoons she began to make friends. She rushed to them immediately, barking in what sounded like pleasure. She had found the breeds with which she belonged. I wondered how. I knew that all the world's dogs belonged to a single species, *Canis familiaris*. Here in the park, where the animals ranged in size and hair type, I couldn't distinguish their significant similarities. I supposed it was something contained within their sniffs or their yaps, or something less obvious, a posture or a gait.

It wasn't until the following week that a distant wall of stacked shipping containers on the far side of the park caught my attention. This must have once been some sort of depot. Looking again, I noticed that several containers had been repurposed as dwelling spaces, and not in the stylishly architectural way that I had seen attempted in other countries. The walls of the rusting, listing boxes had been simply, but unevenly, cut open for doors and windows. Tattered nylon tents dotted the perimeter elsewhere around the site. There were worse places to live than the former printing factory. I didn't see any of their actual residents.

Shaking off the sense that I was being watched from inside the containers, I mingled with the other dog owners. I asked them what kind of dogs they had and immediately forgot their answers, but I felt that I had at least introduced myself.

Within several weeks the containers had seemed to recede into the haphazard enclave surroundings and I gradually became more comfortable there. This feeling of comfort was again short-lived.

One afternoon, on a day that was warm and sunny, I threw the ball, my dog caught it, and she brought it back with another dog trailing her. A woman came up to the second dog and rubbed his neck fur.

"Ron," she said, looking up. She was wearing a purple stretchy top and a loose matching skirt, what I think was once called athleisure wear, though in the district adults enjoyed limited opportunities for either athletics or leisure. When I didn't immediately respond, she said, "It's me. You know, from high school." She added, "Nikisha Jones."

She made a joke about how she must look different in daylight. I made a little embarrassed remark too, about being a basement-dwelling creature whose eyes were ill adapted for the sun. I looked around for Buster. She saw the gesture and shook her head.

I told her how my dog had been a stray found in a parking lot. She said that was how most migrants acquired pets.

Our dogs seemed pleased to have found each other, if that's what the wagging of their tails represented. Mine took off and Nikisha's chased her, yapping, snout nearly against snout. Then mine stopped and ran after Nikisha's. We watched their good-natured romp, not really knowing what a social encounter meant for a dog or what the dogs meant to each other. The dogs eventually began wrestling, kicking up clouds of dirt. This was accompanied by happy barks, squeals, snaps, yips, and more yaps, but then I heard what sounded like my dog's angry growl.

I clapped my hands and called her by her name. She stopped playing/fighting as if she had been waiting for my call. She came to me, her friend following.

"That's my girl," I said, scratching behind her ears. I repeated her name. "Good girl!"

Nikisha was patting her own dog, but watching me alertly, as if I might make a sudden move. I understood that her sharp intake of breath through slightly parted lips, her narrowed eyes, and her absolute stillness was an expression of anxious surprise that was familiar to me from another occasion.

"I used to live there," I explained, my nonchalance so careful it was obvious. "A beautiful city, really. It's built right on the water, around a wide bay, but you can see the mountains in the distance. A busy metropolis, a noisy city, lots of commerce, and lots of traffic, everyone simply trying to make a living."

She considered this for a few minutes. The two dogs ran off again, in pursuit of a ball that was thrown to another dog. We watched them as if we had money riding on every bounce, every leap, every grab, and the eventual winner of the contest. She said at last that the city for which my dog was named sounded lovely.

I felt that I had permission to go on.

"It was. I mean, it was also expensive and I never had any money, but I could simply walk the streets and appreciate the medieval architecture and, downtown, the skyscrapers. The glass was constantly changing colors to reflect the shift of light on the bay. The city has an old library, with a reading room under a marbled rotunda, around which narrow windows let in a constant soft glow. Not far from the library there's a cathedral. The square in front is always packed with people coming and going, including colorfully robed priests and nuns. And then there's the folk music. You turn a corner onto a little crooked street and come upon a little orchestra or band that has set up chairs on the cobblestones. What strange instruments, some of them made of shells and hollowed animal bones found in the highlands. A long cement promenade arcs around the bay. The promenade is called the Corniche. It's crowded and lively on nice days. Families, couples. I used to go every Sunday."

She looked away now, beyond the dog park and the chain-link fence, toward a stand of scrawny trees across the road. She was absorbing my words, every last detail.

"I had a friend there," I said. "Someone I loved."

She nodded gravely.

"We used to walk along the Corniche together," I added.

I had gone too far. She pretended not to hear me.

Instead, speaking in a near murmur, she said, "I

also lived in another country before I came here. I had
to leave the States. Things had happened. I eventually
acquired a fake foreign passport and I pretended to
be someone else every minute of the day. But I missed
America, I missed our town. The experience of being
abroad, in exile, was so intense and character changing that I was sure I would forget who I was. The
girl and teenager I had been before the war: that was
already like a dream about someone else. The wife
and mother I became early in the war: a fantasy. So
I hungered for every kind of news about our country,
even news of the most catastrophic kind. I studied the
news as if it were the story of my personal life. I looked
for signs of America everywhere abroad, even if it was
only someone eating a hamburger, even if every part
of the hamburger—the meat, the bun, the toppings—
were wrong."

"Foreigners have strange ideas about what consti-
tutes a hamburger," I noted. "Also bagels. Also General
Tso's chicken."

"I was, I think, a little crazy. I recklessly risked expo-
sure, posing as one person but still devoted to my life as
somebody else. I still thought I could reclaim what I left
behind. That's how desperate I was. I needed to hear
whatever people could tell me about the town I came
from, our town, every recollection of every detail, physical and nonphysical. I wanted to have placed in my ears
the names of the schoolteachers and the names of the

football players, the names of the streets where I learned to drive, the names of the stores in the mall, everything."

I said with some bitterness: "I hope you heard that then."

"Ron," she said urgently. "I did. But also something else. I found a friend. Just like the friend you found. I found someone I could trust. I don't think I would have survived without this friend. I'll never forget this person."

"And now you're here, in the enclave. Not quite America, but something closer than what you had in the other city."

"That's right," she said impenitently. "I've resumed my former American life. My husband had been interned. Then he was released, got away from the States, met me in this country, and we resumed our life together, as difficult as it had been. I've tried to resume my life as if everything I had elsewhere I never had. This is the only sane way to do it, obviously."

After this, we played some more with our dogs. I seemed to find more occasions to call my dog by her name. I mumbled it into her fur. I shouted it across the lot. Buster's wife stood beside me. She no longer flinched at the sound of the name of the city on the bay, accepting its annunciation as if it were a punishment. After a while we parted. I said I'd see her around. She smiled weakly and said it was really a small enclave.

✦

Anonymously performing my inspections, my ears
perked as I passed from basement to basement, I was
more aware than ever of the river of anger that washed
through the district, even if I couldn't precisely locate
its headwaters. People continued to speak of recent
American history, mostly quietly or in private. They
comforted their spouses. They sobbed to their lovers.
They tried to instruct their children. I encountered several more organized storytelling groups, like the one I
had listened to in the basement of the former insurance
company, but with other plotlines and other implications. Nothing I heard was spoken offhand. It was an
urgent transmission of knowledge, a forcefully ham-
mered construction of story, several secret histories. We
would never hold title to a unitary public history. That
was something for future generations to write, though
even then there would be further room for argument.

I heard enough to understand the cries of grievance
and also to recognize, within the cries, repeated often,
the name of a single locality that had for some years been
central to the hostilities. The name belonged to our
town. As I had already been reminded, as if I needed
reminding, our ordinary town in the heart of America
had inflicted and suffered mass roundups, beatings, and
torture. It was famous. Certain measures had been taken
across the community, in private homes, and in public

offices—and in the former bowling alley, for instance. People spoke of these places in dread. The place I continued to hear referred to most often was still the abandoned Target store on the county road. I must have passed the store thousands of times before the conflict. I worked there once for a few weeks over the Christmas holidays. The Target now came up repeatedly.

This was when I thought, if I listened closely enough, that I heard the name of Amanda Keller again, pronounced more audibly, more emphatically, and more precisely. The name was expressed within a penumbra of awe and hatred that I could hardly bear to believe had come to surround the quiet girl from my high school physics class.

I then suddenly became very busy. A temporary power outage across the enclave had disabled some of the equipment, which had to be reprogrammed in one basement after another. I was out late every night, deeply involved in my work, no longer gathering intelligence, except unconsciously. This was a relief. A few units, their circuits scrambled, required very close attention. I stopped thinking, mostly, about what had happened at home. I was nevertheless aware, from what I heard and observed in the street, that the competition between the enclave's criminal gangs had now become more contentious. The original political arguments were being amplified.

I knew too that there was talk of an independent commission that would investigate the recent sorrows that had bloodied American soil. It would be composed of distinguished jurists from around the world, people said. At first I assumed the panel was something new, another short-lived international effort to bring peace and justice to the region. This idea was floated every few years, with the nominal acceptance of the warring American parties who then slow-walked their cooperation. I soon realized, however, that the panel would be the same fact-finding commission that had been established years ago while I was living in the city on the bay. That commission had apparently completed a significant amount of research, visiting incident sites and taking testimony in America and abroad, before the withdrawal of international support shut it down.

The commission's potential resumption wasn't reported in the enclave's English-language media, where it might have been seen as inflammatory. I could glean only bits and pieces from my imperfect reading of the native press. It was not yet decided, if the commission was reconvened, whether the national government, whose country hosted the largest American population abroad, would support it. Much would depend on the international climate, as well as domestic politics, which had recently become complicated. One of the native parties now seemed more allied with one of the American sides, though the issues that roiled local politics weren't remotely like our own.

The detective seemed offended when I asked about

the commission, as if the question had disrupted the normal relations between policeman and informer. He had met me that morning on the broken sidewalk under a dark highway overpass, blocking my way. All I could really make out was the glow of his smoking-tube. Water dripped somewhere. He said he didn't know anything about the commission. He said the media lied anyway.

He was more interested in the heightened conflict between the enclave's criminal organizations and was frustrated by my inability to tell him anything specific: names, places, actual evidence of conflict. I said it was only a feeling. I had been focused on my work. I added, however, that if the American militias became involved in national politics, their dispute could spill outside the enclave.

"Don't worry about what happens outside the enclave," he snapped.

"Do you think the government will accept the commission? Will they let them call on Americans?"

"I don't know," he insisted. "But if they come they'll subpoena Americans. That's the point."

"Is the government going to fall? Or is something else happening? Something worse? I don't understand the politics."

The detective said, "Just do me a favor, Ron Patterson, wake up. Try to pay attention to what's happening *here*, in the district. Don't worry about the politics. This isn't your country."

His declaration stung me, surprisingly. Of course it

wasn't my country. I could hardly speak more than a few words of the language. I didn't know any native people, except for him. I didn't know their food, their music, their religion, or their history. I had never been inside a native home. My permission to live in this country was no more than tentative.

It was nevertheless the place I lived, perhaps the only place I could. I suppose I had developed an attachment.

✦

I biked to one of the schools late in the afternoon after most of the students had left. We had received reports of a software anomaly. Even with its corridors empty, the building, a former refrigerator factory, still reminded me of an ordinary American high school. Instructional posters lined the walls. Olive-green lockers had been installed. Somewhere the school band was practicing. It evidently had a way to go before it reached proficiency.

A few classrooms were located in a large basement area that was subdivided without a hallway. One room let into another. Checking my map, I passed through an English classroom, where I took note of the portraits of once-famous authors and their once-famous, once-meaningful quotes. I came then to a social studies classroom lined by bookcases. A few framed or matted maps were scattered around the room, maps of the United

States and the world, impossibly dated, of course, now that so many borders had been redrawn.

My equipment was installed at the far end of the next room, in the same corner as some mechanical paraphernalia that identified the classroom as belonging to the science department. I carefully pushed aside the devices and opened the panel. I ran a few tests and saw that I would have to replace a faulty circuit board.

Once I did that and closed up, I carefully moved back the science equipment, some of which was familiar from my own high school physics class, bits and pieces of apparatus: balsa dowels, brushed-steel rods, loose springs, ceramic armatures, dials, knobs, a shoebox with a lens fixed in a hole at one end, and several scratched but otherwise intact mirrors in a variety of light-bending forms. Mr. Strauss had used this kind of equipment in demonstrations of important physical principles. He thought that understanding these principles, or rather the entire framework of scientific inquiry, was more urgent than ever that year. He stressed the roles of observation and reason in thinking about the world we lived in. He tended to repeat himself. He sometimes seemed despairing.

I identified the wave generator first. It was an apparatus about two feet long and lined with an assembly of flexible rods of various lengths fixed to a wire. The machine was designed to replicate several kinds of transverse waves, like ocean and electromagnetic waves. It could also be manipulated to demonstrate wave reflection, wave resonance, and constructive and destructive wave interference. Perhaps unintentionally, the movement of the waves to and fro created a hypnotic effect, though one insufficient to instill the actual lessons in our minds.

I picked up the shoebox and looked in through a slit on the opposite side of the lens. I had made something like this in Mr. Strauss's class. A sheet of translucent wax paper had been fixed inside the box. It was difficult to find the paper's proper placement, which was determined by the focal length of the double-convex lens. I had tested it repeatedly, pointing the device at other students, Mr. Strauss, and the light fixtures. When I finally had the screen correctly adjusted, I turned to look at a girl in the back of the room. She was engrossed in constructing her own device. Her image inside my box was insubstantial, unsteady, translucently ectoplasmic, reversed. The name of the device now glimmered before me for a few moments: *camera obscura.*

The mirrors had been employed in the same series of lessons that began with the idea that, as Mr. Strauss put it, "we don't see anything directly. Each thing we think we see, every living organism and every inanimate object, is a manifestation of the light that has either emanated from the object or been reflected by the object." He declared, "This light can be manipulated." He showed us how, employing concave and convex mirrors, plano-convex and convexo-concave lenses, and other optical tools. He demonstrated how the concave mirror in a reflecting tele-scope enlarged and inverted the image; we experimented with focal lengths that progressively increased the mag-nification. He explained that what was seen in a flat plane mirror was a "virtual image," in which the image of the object appeared to be positioned, impossibly, behind the mirror's surface. Yet the image was reversed from left to right because *we* seemed to be standing behind the object, looking through it from the back.

"Remember," he said. "The world is real. The world is a fact. To reach that fact, however, you have to recog-nize how our tools of perception operate, how they're limited, what they distort, what they amplify, what they diminish, and what they leave out. But the fact is there."

I now picked up a concave mirror and held it so that it looked behind me over my shoulder. Until I steadied the glass, the image hurtled through space, coming at me sharp and close. The field of view settled on a stack of identical textbooks outside the room, at the far end of the social studies classroom, their spines outward, right at my fingertips. I read the title:

PROBLEMS IN AMERICAN HISTORY

An object was dislodged from my memory, not by the books, but by the preceding sensation of occupying a spinning room. And then the image had loomed, an illu-sion of closeness and tangibility. I had experienced this disorientation several times during those lessons years ago when we fooled around with Mr. Strauss's optical instruments. Every time, it seemed, I turned to look at the same girl in the back of the classroom, a person at the instrument's object of focus, an individual who I never knew or really looked at without the mediation of optical glass. Her image was and always would be reversed or magnified or in some way put into question. Her name was not Nikisha, of course. I now carefully put down the apparatus and took my toolbox. I returned through the empty social studies and English classrooms, turning off the lights.

✦

I checked out a company van so that I could inspect some equipment in the neighboring province, a five-hour drive north. The two-lane road left directly from the enclave, bypassing the city, and traffic was very light. The road passed unproductive or marginally agricultural land and went through a few scattered settlements. Not long after I left I was stopped at a traffic check by the police. They examined my papers and waved me on my way. I encountered the police again an hour later. The third checkpoint was operated by the military. The soldiers were no less correct in their bearing, but they slung vintage rifles over their shoulders. I thought I detected an undercurrent of anxiety. They were very meticulous as they checked the back of the vehicle.

This coastal region, I understood, was politically

restive, either because of ethnic differences that I myself couldn't distinguish, or something religious or historical or linguistic or having to do with lifestyle choice. It had been in the news, anyway. The deepening, broadening political crisis was said to have originated here.

The hamlet I eventually reached was dispersed around the highway, which was lined on either side of the road by a widely spaced series of single-level homes constructed in a local style that I had never seen before. There was also a stretch of attached shops that included a post office. The shops were apparently open, but I didn't see either salespeople or customers inside. The houses showed no signs of their inhabitants. Their shades were down. I parked the van on the side of the road and followed my map to units on the roofs of three small buildings. I ran some tests. Although the equipment was running normally, I switched out one circuit board that seemed to be nearing the end of its usable life. These inspections took about an hour. From the roofs I could savor the tang of an ocean breeze, though I couldn't see the ocean itself.

When I came back down to the street five or six small children, all girls less than ten, were waiting there. They were the first people I had encountered in the hamlet. As I approached, on my way to the van, the girls shyly huddled on the sidewalk for protection. Their eyes were wide and their stares never left me.

"Hey, kids, how are you?" I said in the local language.

This set off an explosion of giggles and the two smallest girls left their places to hide behind the others.

A relatively tall girl remained in front, the boldest of them. She studied me in grim solemnity.

She eventually said, "Who are you?"

"My name is Ron. What's *your* name?"

The other girls were again amazed to hear the strange creature speak, in an approximation of their own language no less. They giggled some more. The tall, serious girl told me her name, but I couldn't quite catch it.

She demanded, "Where do you come from?"

"The United States," I said. "Of America."

The girl repeated, "America!" Her friends echoed this with shrieks and sighs of wonder and then imitated what I said several times among themselves. They chattered beyond my comprehension. The girl who had been conducting the interview took a few moments to consider my origins. She then suddenly broke into a broad smile. She exclaimed, "Soybeans!"

I laughed. Mostly because of the self-inflicted destruction of its economy, and also as a matter of international law, the United States exported very few products these days. Of course, virtually no industrial goods were made in the States anymore. The few items that were still manufactured remained under export sanctions that limited the flow of resources to the combatants. The world gladly deprived itself of American cars, planes, weapons, and pharmaceuticals. It did, however, accept what was left of our agricultural output and the expanding global cattle industry seemed to have an insatiable need for the American soybean. Even in a ravaged land, the three-bean pods grew fast and were easily harvested for export, where it was turned mostly into beef, but also into ingredients for processed bread, yogurt, cheese, peanut butter, and chocolate. Furthermore, soybean oil was an everyday component of plastic, building insulation, and glue. "Yes, soybeans!" I confirmed.

An elderly man ambled out of the nearest home, wondering about the excitement that had come to his sleepy outpost. Two of the girls rushed at him to say that I was an American and that I knew how to talk. He smiled at this news and waved his cane. I waved back.

He approached, speaking more quickly than I could understand. I interrupted to explain that my knowledge of the language was very basic. He repeated himself more loudly. Grinning, I told him the name of the company for which I worked and that I had just checked some equipment. I asked if any of the children were his. Two were his granddaughters, he said proudly, and the tall one was his niece. He spoke at further length and after a while I realized that he was inviting me to his home. The niece more patiently repeated the invitation.

I promptly accepted. The man clapped his hands in pleasure. He and the girls brought me around the back of the house into a kitchen where two kerchiefed women were cutting vegetables and stirring pots. They were agog, no less astonished by my arrival than the girls had been. When the man announced that the American would be having dinner with the family, they made noises to the effect that this outlandish declaration was typical of the crazy old man, but they welcomed me warmly and set out an extra plate. I couldn't speak well enough to politely demure, and in any case I was delighted.

Objectively speaking, the food was disgusting. It involved unknown body parts from an unknown animal, floating in a heavy cream sauce, but I ate every bite with a show of appetite. It was washed down with a viscous grog. The girls crowded around me at the table, tittering at what they considered my clumsy use of the country's traditional utensils (in fact, for a foreign person, I was fairly dexterous). The family did most of the speaking, about what I wasn't sure, but I smiled and praised the meal.

When we were done and we had accomplished the ceremonial gestures that signaled the end of the meal, I stood to leave. I thanked them again. Rather than take me out the back, the man accompanied me through the house to the door facing the street. We went past bedrooms and rooms whose purposes were unclear. I made admiring sounds, trying to remember everything, including the layout. The home's interior was like nothing I had ever imagined, yet it was also sufficiently recognizable. A bed was a bed. A lamp was a lamp. The walls were occupied with family photographs, old movie posters, rug coverings, and what looked like an amateur watercolor, which displayed a bowl of distinctive native fruit.

He caught me staring at one of the posters. The print was dominated by a very famous movie star. I was stopped in my tracks.

He said, "I love foreign films!"

"Me too," I murmured.

"You've seen it? They showed it in America?"

"Of course they did. I like the actor. He's a good actor. I'm not sure this was his best effort, though."

"What?" he said. He seemed stunned. Even the girls were surprised. The man then delivered a forceful argument, most of which I didn't understand. He told me that this film had made him the person he was today. It had shaped the direction of his life. Although the story was set in a very different country, very far away, featuring characters who apparently had nothing in common with him, hardly a day went by when a scene from the film—a stray piece of dialogue, a look exchanged by the actors, something glimpsed at the edge of the screen—didn't come to mind with immediate personal relevance. The man appeared to have been offended by my offhand remark.

"Of course it's a great film," I said hurriedly. I wondered now whether he was correct and whether I was simply being obstinate, for several decades now, in not liking the film. The badness of the movie was an untestable proposition, like so many other propositions, including those related to politics and personal relationships. Yet it seemed to me like something more than an opinion; really, it was as close to a fact as an untestable proposition could be, and it was a view widely accepted by the world's filmgoing public, I thought. But it was still not a fact. My host hardly seemed mollified, so I added, "I was just joking with you, like we Americans do. It may very well be the best film ever made. I've seen it many times."

He slapped me on the back.

The entire family walked me to the van, joined by neighbors who had observed the unfamiliar vehicle and learned that a foreign person, an American, had come to the settlement. They all wanted to see. The small girls stayed close. Their discovery of the stranger had given them ownership. I opened the door to the van. My host kissed me and we embraced, as was the custom. I promised to come back.

I was elated by my first real contact with the ordinary people of this country. They had been so kind, I thought. They had shown me hospitality. The children were no less good-natured, and no less hilarious, than the American children that I walked among when I visited the enclave's schools. I'd have to check the equipment again next year. By then I would speak their language more easily. Also, I would find a shop in the enclave that sold American-style candy. The children would find the candy strange—perhaps the idea of candy would itself be strange to them—but I was sure they'd scarf it down anyway, the imitation Smarties, the imitation Snickers, and the imitation Skittles.

✦

In the next few weeks, now that I had seen with my own
eyes the country beyond the enclave, the district seemed
more cramped and more limited than ever. The marsh-
lands were not so vast. You could reach the end of the
district in a single bike ride or see it whole from the top
floor of one of the indigenous religious towers that had
been converted to residences, its mirrored glass orna-
mentation mostly still in place. The isolated enclave
seemed immured within the American past, fated to
keep its customs and its bigotries, fated to rewrite the
same tragedies, and a few comedies too. I saw the same
people more often, which made me wonder how many
Americans lived in the district anyway. Given the political
sensitivities, those figures may have been classified.

Biking down one small, quiet commercial street,
I saw Buster on the sidewalk up ahead. It was too late
to turn around. He was at a shop with a big plate glass
window, in front of which he was casually speaking
with some men; these were probably the same men who
were with him before. The shop's signage declared that
the business had something to do with graphic design:
advertising and brochures, I supposed. There might
have been a growing demand for that kind of work,
though I also guessed that the store was at least a sub-
sidiary of some larger, less-benign enterprise. The militias all operated casinos, but they seemed to be involved

with graphic design in one way or another as well. They made documents.

His smile faded as I approached. With a shudder of foreboding, I tentatively lifted my arm from the handlebar. He raised his too, in reflexive greeting, while he contemplated me with a hard, direct gaze. I had to stop, but I stayed on my bike, straddling it.

"Ron Patterson," I said.

"I know who you are."

I tried to think of some pleasantries to exchange, but the weather these past few days had been utterly featureless.

He said slowly, "It's remarkable that you once knew my wife. That you went to the same school, that you lived in the same town."

"I don't think we ever spoke to one another," I insisted. He hadn't used his wife's name. Neither would I. It might have suggested the fragility of the fiction. It could have made me a threat to be quashed. "Or that we had any of the same friends."

He was dissatisfied with my response, but he changed the direction of the conversation. Still trying to determine my loyalties, he wanted to know where I had been after I left the States and how I had lived. I would never have thought to say that this was none of his business, even if he wasn't accompanied by his men, who stood on either side of me. I gave him the full history, refuge by refuge, semi-menial job by semi-menial job, year by year, except that I slightly fudged the years. I thought it was prudent for this accounting not to include the city on the bay.

He seemed ready to let me go. I smiled and said it was a pleasure chatting with them. I put a foot on one of the pedals and was about to push off, but then I said:

"You know what I miss most about America?"

Surprised that I wasn't taking the immediate opportunity to leave, he said, "What?"

I had seized his men's attention. There was so much to miss about America, a vanished landscape once occupied by structures trivial and meaningful, consumer items and deeply held societal values, daily commutes and cherished ways of life. They were impossible to replicate now that their foundations were gone. The memories of certain common American experiences wouldn't survive the currently living generation. Buster's men were now privately assembling their own lists.

"Baseball," I declared.

Buster looked at me blankly. The other men may not have been old enough to have ever seen an organized game.

"Yes, baseball!" I said. "I played in right for the high school team, totally second-string, but I loved to hit and field. I used to watch the pros on TV, I studied the box scores. I couldn't get enough of it, really. They had the sport in other countries, of course, but that was something truly American, almost like an American folk custom. Did you ever play?"

He shook his head. His gesture suggested distrust, which I pretended not to notice. I smiled cheerfully, not that his lack of interest in the game gave me comfort, and I biked away.

✦

A few days later the country was rocked by news from the northern province. Student protests closed a technical college and the national government summoned the army. The troops had virtually no training in handling civil unrest. Four students were killed in a two-day riot and the brutally clumsy efforts to restore order. The enclave's English-language media only summarily reported the events, which played out not far from the settlement I had visited.

Like most Americans, I was hardly impressed either by the degree of disturbance or by the number of fatalities. In the States, of course, deadly violence had been for some time a daily item in the forecast of the political weather. Many other countries had become accustomed to it too. Our hosts, however, had known centuries of harmony. They believed they were essentially in agreement on their reading of the nation's history and on the state of present-day society. So, for many people, the intensity of the demonstrations and the harshness of the response came out of the blue.

This shock was amplified by the minute-by-minute,

on-the-scene news coverage. The national media also closely reported the reactions of the country's profoundly distressed leaders, opposition figures, and ordinary citizens. I spent part of that week doing inspections outside the enclave, in the city, where the story was tracked by every screen I encountered, on buildings, on billboards, on bus shelters, in subway cars, and in warm, damp hands. In the faces of passersby I saw sorrow and fear and whatever grimaces and sighs might have indicated indigenous hand-wringing and soul-searching. I encountered people on street corners in furious, painful argument with each other or simply in tears. Every student who died received a lengthy, poignant, potentially heartbreaking obituary. It was reported, however, that one of them had acquired a gun, alarming news in a country where virtually no civilians had guns. It was never fired, but one of the young soldiers lost his sight after being hit by a bottle. His story, remarkable in its own way, was given a full telling. The more exhaustive the reporting, the more readers wondered whether they even knew their country. Although they had recognized certain differences among their people, few thought these differences mattered—even among some who were disadvantaged by these differences. The depth of feeling by those who now identified themselves as belonging to one side was a surprise to those who found themselves relegated to the other, many of whom resented the designation. Some of that resentment began to turn militant.

Like most of us in the enclave, I found these divisions immaterial, especially compared to the ones that had riven American history, arguments that swam in our blood and were carved in our bones, even if you were not the least bit political. The local grievances were risible, we thought. As far as we knew, you couldn't even tell the sides apart, not from looking at them, though I suppose they employed certain secondary signifiers visible to those who cared. For the most part, we Americans thought the native people should just ignore trivialities and get on with their lives. After all, they had a pretty nice country.

The affair preoccupied the nation for weeks, complicating the already difficult relations between the political parties. As the story developed, new facts emerged or were reemphasized and once-forgotten (or repressed) chapters in the country's history were recalled. Perceptions shifted one way and then reversed themselves. The debate narrowed in on the question of culpability for the violence. Neither of the main political parties had encouraged the protests, both had denounced the violence, and both expressed grief over the loss of life—though it seemed that one side could be framed as being more sympathetic to the issues raised by the protesters, an affinity the other side tried to exploit, but overenthusiastically, provoking a reaction. One side, but not necessarily the side of the government, could also be blamed for the unpreparedness of the troops. By the end of the month, once public opinion had settled, the tragedy seemed to have been charged to the opposition's account, as far as I could tell.

None of this had anything to do with the enclave's American community, at least not directly, at least not logically. None of the issues being disputed had any connection to American politics. The history didn't resonate with any elements of ours. We were keenly aware, however, that our position in this country depended on obscure political mechanics, like something unseen inside a gearbox. They whirred, they ticked. The enclave's criminal organizations were aware of these wheelworks. The militias had local patrons outside the enclave. These patrons had agendas. The patrons of their rivals had agendas too. The machinery ground away.

✦

Not every structure in the overpopulated enclave was made available to the migrants. The government had shut tight the abandoned local municipal office building, perhaps in the expectation that the district would someday be reclaimed, even gentrified. Its security equipment still needed to be inspected, of course. The front doors were chained, but I had the master key, and the doors were triple-locked, but the key worked for them too. I encountered several more locked doors inside the building. The key opened them all. I burrowed down into the building's lower floors until I reached the last locked room to get to an equipment panel that hadn't been replaced in years, according to the call sheet.

The lights weren't working, so I attached to the edge of the open door a battery-powered lamp, which infused the windowless room with a poisonous yellow glow. This must have been some kind of office, probably for the lowliest of municipal workers. A row of cleared desks occupied the center of the room. Filing cabinets were arranged along one wall, each drawer labeled in the characteristically tidy native hand. A faded, fly-specked map of the district was posted on the opposite wall. It was the same map as the pocket-size one I carried, but it depicted a neighborhood not yet touched by the American way of life, or the American idea, or the American misfortune.

The panel was blocked. Three towers of cardboard file boxes were unevenly piled in front of it, almost ready to topple. I put down my toolbox and moved the cartons one at a time, restacking them in the center of the room. I wondered who had put them there. Unlike the file cabinets, the boxes weren't labeled. They were tied with twine. Annoyed that the cartons had been placed against the unit—in disregard of all regulations—I may have been careless, pulling on the twine to lift them. The string around one of the boxes broke and the carton fell to the floor, spilling its contents. Another carton toppled over and split.

I left the files while I worked on the panel. I replaced the circuit board and ran several tests. Dissatisfied with the results, I removed the board. I scraped some contacts and reinserted it. This was an exacting, tiring task in the dim light.

When I was done, I was reminded that the files were still scattered on the floor, half-escaped from their manila folders. Bending over, I saw at once that they weren't printed in the local language, but rather in several foreign languages, including English. I scooped up a stack. Certain seals and stationery headings indicated that they were official documents of some kind. They were dated from several years earlier. I looked at them for a few moments. Then, as if fearful that I was being watched, I urgently shoved the papers back in the cartons and retied the boxes with the torn twine.

I locked up and went home to walk my dog. That night I lay in my cot and thought hard about what I had seen so briefly, trying to recall in particular the names of the organizational entities that had been stamped at the top of each document. A "brigade." A "unit." A "resistance group." The embossments indicated that the files were compiled abroad well before I had come to the enclave. The cartons had evidently been brought to the district and dumped in the basement, hurriedly, perhaps recently. I wondered by whom. Few people would have had access to the building. I wondered, too, about who else knew the cartons were there.

Testimony had been taken, information had been collected, and interim reports were written, with places and dates and casualty figures. Evidence had been saved incompletely, possibly in haste, in less than ideal conditions. I wanted nothing to do with this evidence, nor with anyone who had hidden these files there. I didn't want to know how the documents had been obtained and what purposes they had been assigned. Yet the little I had seen played on my mind, its language formidably legalistic and its toponymy mostly but not entirely unfamiliar. The casualty figures were higher than I would have guessed.

✦

I knew that I would have to be careful. Filing a report that the unit was about to fail, I generated an open service ticket. Another inspection appeared on my call sheet within a week.

I brought a second light with me this time, as well as some fresh twine. After entering the room, I locked the door behind me. The cartons were where I had left them, untouched since my last visit.

After checking the equipment—out of habit and a sense of obligation—I reopened the carton that had spilled the previous week. I flipped through the manila folders.

I pulled the next box from the pile and cut the twine with my utility knife. It too was jammed with files.

Their tabs were labeled according to some arcane system, employing proper names, dates, and other letters and figures that weren't recognizable to me, but all of it was American. The people who had put together these files had done it methodically. Every carton contained a master file in which every file within the box was listed and cross-referenced. I went through them one by one. By the time I found the name I was looking for—even though I was looking for it, the name jumped out like a sliver of glass and stuck me in the eye—the cartons were scattered around the room, nearly every top removed.

Amanda Keller's file was cross-referenced with the name of my hometown, cross-referenced too with a name that was *not* Buster Williams, and cross-referenced yet again with the name of a militia. The file was not as full as the others in the carton, most of which were generated by our region of the state, but it was nevertheless substantial. Her middle name was Dickerson. Her parents' names were Richard (deceased) and Donna (deceased). She had been born two months after me and had lived only a few blocks away, I learned. The documents' identifying information included her driver's license and Social Security numbers, and more obscure figures collected from her social media and internet use, as well as certain biometric indicators. The commission had been very thorough. It had even collected her high school transcript. I noted with some irritation that Mr. Strauss had given her an A.

She had fled the States. Amanda's movements across several foreign countries were reconstructed up to her discovery by local police authorities cooperating with the investigative commission. She had been summoned as a witness. The hearing site was reserved, the lawyers were assembled, the stenographer was hired, the translator was hired, a Bible was procured. Then the commission lost the support of the local national government and its international backers. It was disbanded. She never testified. That was why her file was relatively light. Her next whereabouts were unknown, her trail gone cold.

Other people's testimony occupied the bulk of the file, pages upon pages of questions and responses from witnesses interviewed in the States and abroad. I flipped through them, tripping over town landmarks and the names of several witnesses, individuals I had known personally. Certain sentences were long and contained multiple clauses. Some were simply declarative. I would have to read every one of them.

But first I went back to the top sheet to check the date of her scheduled hearing, which would have taken place in an antipodal city squeezed between a wind-churned ocean bay and a range of mountains famous for their network of hiking trails. The date was years ago, of course, years that had for me mostly flickered by in a blur. I worked my way backward from my time in the enclave, my year at sea, back through one country and then another, back through my tenure at the food-processing plant, and then a little further. I was unsurprised when I landed in the year of the hearing. With more effort, crouched over the cartons in the subbasement, I recalled the months of that year, one at a time. I confirmed, still unsurprised, that the commission had been disbanded only weeks before Marlise rescued me from the antimigrant march.

I REMAINED IN THE crouching position long after it had become painful. I must have wanted it to be painful, especially after another name in the files, interred halfway down a certain list, lit up a room elsewhere, as if in a blaze. In that room a lengthy journey was being undertaken, in a remote country, in a distant decade. The kids had piled into the school bus, shouting and shoving, competing over who would sit with whom, and our teachers, increasingly out of patience, ordered the still-standing students into the vacant seats. I was put next to a girl I only vaguely knew. I was a ninth-grade boy, in all my ninth-grade boyness. The echoing clamor within the bus receded as if down a tunnel. My vision narrowed. A wave of heat washed over me, sticky and penetrating. The girl asked if I was allergic to peanuts. No, shellfish, I stammered. She spent a long time looking at the back of a bag of candy. No shellfish, she said at last. She aimed the opening of the bag in my general direction. I ignored it for a while until, still staring hard at the back of the yellow bus parked in front of ours, I reached in and withdrew a single M&M. Our bus finally started its engine.

The other young travelers continued to behave rambunctiously, but we didn't take part in the rambunction, neither of us sitting near our friends. After some time the girl, who was apparently not suffering as much as I was, asked if I liked a certain band. I was aware, of course, that she had launched a conventional conversational gambit, but I was astounded by her capacity to do so. Also, by the fact that she thought I deserved a gambit. I was further amazed that I was capable of responding. As it happened, I did like the band, or at least I was familiar with it.

By any adult standards, the conversation was superficial and desultory, but we managed to sustain it for the next thirty or forty minutes. We moved on to films, to television shows, and to the gross singularities of our teachers. For me the exchange was a revelation, swinging open a door to a future in which I would have many such dialogues: idle, friendly. Even the long pauses in our conversation seemed ordinary and we waited patiently for them to end.

The girl and I were separated once we reached our destination, a planetarium in a small museum complex. She actually said, have fun, and I actually said, you too. I rejoined my friends, who still kidded around, but in the darkened auditorium, surrounded by the great bug-like machine bristling with mirrors and lenses, I felt myself immersed within a deep, space-like quiet. The girl was somewhere else in the auditorium, of course, but not visible in the feeble light cast by the imitation stars and planets. She returned to school with her friends in the other bus.

A second familiar name appeared in the same necrology: Buster Williams.

NOW I HAD TO stand. Now I had to stretch my legs. I had to run too, but instead I opened the panel again to check the perfectly functioning equipment. The sub-basement's dampness began to penetrate my clothes. The boxes were still uncovered.

I would never surpass the hourly income I earned during the Christmas shopping season that I worked at our hometown Target. The store was among the chain's largest in the region, the grocery department virtually below the horizon as seen from someone standing in the bedding section. I came in before the store opened and swept my broom through what seemed like a pregnant stillness. The shoppers were gathering beyond the sliding glass doors. Once they were allowed to enter, in an exuberant rush that suggested release and determination, I was sent from one section to the other as needed. I occasionally led the customers to more specialized Team Members, especially in Electronics.

I also worked in the back storage area. Delivery trucks slid the containers directly into the bays. The

pallets on which the goods rested were moved by fork-
lifts that I wasn't allowed to operate. They were stocked
in large storage cages that ascended nearly to the corru-
gated metal roof. The stacks stretched from one end of
the storage area to the other.

These cages, I learned as I turned the pages of the
files, would later be employed to hold men and women,
twenty to a cage, in increasingly filthy conditions.
Food and water would be supplied irregularly. To ease
overcrowding, the second level of cages would eventually be occupied as well. After a fight broke out at the
latrines, malnourished and ill prisoners would no longer be brought outside to use them. Feces, urine, and
vomit would flow freely into the ground-floor cages from
the cages above their inhabitants' heads. In the holiday
weeks in which I worked at Target, when the cages were
piled with dehumidifiers, multipiece linen sets, and flat-
screen TVs, while the distant cries of the national news
were rising into a single, full-throated howl, I may have
had an intimation that something like this would eventually happen.

I may have known too that the vinyl composition
flooring in the Housewares section, underneath the
College Living Shop sign, would someday be smeared
with blood. So would the tiles in Sporting Goods and
Travel. These crimson, lilac, and pink streaks, even after
they were subjected to bleach and lye, would remain in
the flooring for years, during which copious samples

would be scraped up by several occasionally competing investigating authorities.

The light in the subbasement was really too weak for reading.

A NATION MAY FALL into crisis, millions may lose work, and tens of thousands may resort to arms, but the Department of Motor Vehicles abides. I was reminded now that my friend Ravi had driven me to the mostly shuttered state office complex, past a police checkpoint, so that I could have my picture taken and receive my first driver's license. It was another half step forward in my unsteady march toward an uncertain adulthood. Ravi was uncomfortable waiting in the lot for me: there were too many men with guns. He accompanied me into the building, which was ostensibly still neutral territory.

I continue to carry this first license, long expired, the only American driver's license I ever had. It still comes in handy from time to time for the purposes of identification. When the card was first placed in my hand I already knew that this permission to drive an automobile was most significant for its identifying powers, which were already ramifying through databases of which I could be only dimly aware. Companies, government agencies, and organizations that were neither would trade this data between themselves, shouting about it in long windowless halls, murmuring log-ins in paneled boardrooms, haggling over third-party tracking cookies while sipping milky tea in smoky dens, and doing something somewhere within the blink of a cursor.

Torture and murder would prove to be not the only tools of conquest, according to a single faint page of confession muttered by a dying inkjet printer, now in my hands. Driver's licenses and other documents were confiscated. Databases were accessed, often with the enthusiastic cooperation of those in authority. Identities could then be appropriated, for all the historically lucrative reasons and also to diminish the number of partisans that could be counted on one side or the other. Also, fresh papers could be manufactured for these identities once one's former documentation became toxic. Some of these recycled identities had belonged to men and women separated from existence, present now only on lists summing up their nonexistence.

IN ORDINARY TIMES, CONVENTIONAL married couples argue about conventional household affairs: who will empty the dishwasher, for instance. The husband and wife assuming control of the Target after the initial days of chaos were frequently at loggerheads over matters specific to their time and place: which prisoners needed to be interrogated first, the manner of their interrogation, food distribution, bathroom breaks, the final end of the bathroom breaks, and whether the facility could accept more prisoners. As recorded in the files, many of

these disputes played out before the eyes of their captives and within their hearing.

The husband was considered the more unpredictable
of the two. Survivors reported that during the beatings
he administered himself, he often stopped listening
to the answers that he had so painstakingly elicited.
Before using force, however, he could be friendly with
the prisoners, many of whom he knew personally. He
could wax philosophical and also profane. He made
sure people were getting fed. At the start of each "interview," which the husband called part of a "process"
that he expected would conclude with the detainee's
release, he collegially went over the intelligence with
him or her, sitting side by side at a Target Room & Joy
bridge table, as if they each had an equal interest in getting to the truth.

The wife, who wore ordinary street clothes and
preferred to keep to the shadows of the abandoned big-
box store, seemed to be the militia person who oversaw operations, according to witnesses. She would be
at the center of the whispered arguments among colleagues. She made the phone calls to the higher-ups.
She once rushed into the parking lot to refuse a delivery of captured enemy fighters. Her husband trailed
her, protesting that it was just one more busload. The
wife was the only person who could intervene once the
beatings became pointless and even then she wasn't
always effective against the force of his temper. Often

the prisoners had to wait for his temper to exhaust itself, especially when she was absent. The couple had a small child at home. It was difficult at that time to arrange for reliable childcare.

Numerous prisoners reported an especially animated marital dispute that was contested just out of hearing in the Clearance department. It was unclear whether the subject was military or domestic, but the disagreement was heated and, as they watched, the prisoners may have reflected upon their own fraught conjugal relationships or the more general problems of human connection. They were perhaps not unembarrassed. The wife was trying to calm the man down. He looked hard at the floor, listening but not liking what he heard. The prisoners initially thought she had successfully made her case. Then he exploded in anger. She again patiently explained her position. He couldn't accept it, although it was obviously the correct position, grounded in objective fact, most of the prisoners concluded, crediting her composure.

They could see the toll the conflict (with him, with them) was taking on her. She seemed to age in the course of the conversation and in the end, whatever the issue, she seemed to have lost the argument or it was at least apparent that she had been forced to give in. She stepped away, her face drawn, her gaze unfocused. The prisoners wondered if the man had been right after all.

The fighting in the region didn't abate. Forces hostile

to the Target militia gathered strength. They were better armed and better trained. The husband and wife's organization desperately needed intelligence about the forces arrayed against them: where they were, how many, what kind of weapons. They didn't know which of the prisoners could be helpful.

Two guards, military veterans who had no interrogation experience but thought they knew how to waterboard, accidentally drowned a prisoner. This was witnessed by the other detainees, whose accounts were consistent. They erupted in fury, pounding on the bars of their cages and flinging feces. Both the vets were sent off, despite the manpower shortage. This didn't end the prisoners' anger. They promised retribution once they were rescued, which they expected to happen shortly. The husband stood before the cages and made a statement denying that anyone had been drowned. The captives were momentarily silenced by the blatancy of the falsehood. They had seen the drowning with their own eyes: the incident was reflected in a still-intact dome mirror suspended above the loading bay. Even after someone asked about the prisoner's condition, the husband was steadfast in his denial. He said the man was released. Now the rage of the captives reached an almost religious frenzy, but the holding pens remained intact. The woman was close by, watching her husband coldly. The waterboarding may have been something else about which they disagreed.

A single witness reported that the couple embraced only once: a week later, just as a critical interstate highway overpass was taken by their adversaries. They were at the far end of the store, near the checkout. The husband's arms loosely rested on the top of her shoulders, his hands clasped behind her back. His head hung down, resting against her collarbone. Distracted, staring into space, she kissed the top of his head. She may have been in tears. That was the last time anyone saw her in the Target, in the town, or in the country. Days later the opposing militia liberated the store and captured the town's outskirts. The husband and their child were taken into custody. Certain "administrative provisions" were made for the child.

I now recalled a voice emanating from a loudspeaker, from a few years before that. It belonged to some kid on another school's AV squad, his intonation deepened and made almost authoritative at the start of a baseball game as he summoned onto the scrubby, rubbishy field the players of each team, visiting and at home. The names echoed against the school buildings and the one-eighth-full stands. I listened for my own name and its watery reflection. The players on the home team were identified next. Their names had become perhaps one-eighth-familiar to us after several previous matches that season. We thought of our mostly faceless opponents mostly as righties or lefties, and by what position they played—but I remembered the boyish, close-to-quaint name of their first baseman and the pleasure the announcer took in drawing it out.

I went hitless and made a few unremarkable catches in right field. A slow roller to third concluded the game, the last of the season and the last in which I would ever participate. It was a very close play and I intended not to forget it. I watched it from the top step of the visitors' dugout. I saw the home team's third baseman scoop it up, pull it from his glove, and fire a bolt across the diamond. I saw the first baseman, his right arm stretched toward third, toward victory, his glove leaning into the electric arc of the charged particle, the youth yearning for the ball with his foot on the bag, his heel off the bag, only the top of his big toe grazing it. The umpire was no longer observing the baseball's trajectory. He had stopped watching the game. He was crouched by the bag, his entire universe the width and height of the bag, listening. The ball sounded in the glove just as the runner's right foot was about to land. I saw the first baseman full in the face now, the circuit between him and the third baseman closed. Out.

ANOTHER NAME ON ANOTHER list, reporting certain "administrative provisions." The entry read, "Nigel Keller Yamaguchi, age three."

✦

The detective didn't appear in the woods again. At the end of a long, low-ceilinged underground room, I looked up from an open panel, and he wasn't there either. I didn't see him in any back or side alleys. For each anticipated encounter, I prepared another story about the found documents and their contents. Each story contradicted the story that I never delivered. Every time he didn't show I was relieved and then I made up a new story for the next imaginary interview, with new details withheld, others offered. Every story meant something else, putting some identities in focus, obscuring others, and magnifying and minimizing responsibility. I rehearsed minimizing responsibility.

I didn't search for the woman and I wasn't sure why I would want to, but she was on my mind, so I suppose I hoped to see her after all. Then I thought I did, first passing by in an SUV and then walking through a parking lot, though the two women may not have been the same person. The second woman was looking away. I went to the dog park where we had once spoken. I thought I recognized her dog and my dog thought she recognized him too, trotting over to nuzzle. The other animal ignored her and went to an unfamiliar woman. Every time I expected to see the woman I had a different idea of what I would say to her and what would be my tone of voice.

I then stopped bringing my dog to the dog park, preferring an untrafficked half-mile stretch of asphalt next to a dead trickle of a creek, where I supposed the district's previous inhabitants may have once fished with their distinctive, impractical-looking tackle. My dog enjoyed the new things to sniff at the edge of the road, like the grasses and the wildflowers. Where the filthy water could be seen moving, it transported obscure debris. She occasionally thought she recognized something and growled at it.

Here, as elsewhere in my travels across the enclave, I felt the caress of the short hairs on my neck and a pressure behind my eyes that was the physiological manifestation of an awareness that I was being observed. I wasn't sure whether the vantage point was situated in the trees alongside the road or on the other side of the creek, or behind the windows of a multistory former office building in the distance.

Many pairs of eyes could have conceivably been interested in me, but I came to the conclusion that I knew who was watching, so I wasn't surprised when an almost-identifiable woman appeared on the road and allowed her dog to lead her in our direction. I assumed it was the woman I was expecting or hoping for.

"Nikisha Jones," I said; as if.

We walked for a while without speaking, our dogs happily accompanying us side by side. The afternoon was coming to a close, but the sky above the creek was still bright. At the place where the road spun away from the creek, we turned and walked back.

Without prompting and without any kind of pre-amble, she began talking about high school. She had always looked forward to the annual student theater production, without ever taking part. We went through the shows year by year: *West Side Story*, *Fiddler*, *Les Miz* (all of which, come to think of it, involved communal violence). She recalled a dreamy history teacher who was often seen with a stylish young French teacher, both of them married. She had put the couple under surveil-lance but had never been able to establish that they were having an affair. She wanted to know whether I thought the assistant principal was gay. Did I remember the fire drill that ended with someone setting a real fire in the boys bathroom? By the time the trucks came and the all clear was sounded, nearly the entire student body had decided to cut the rest of the day.

Now I privately recalled something else, not from the grounds of the high school, but from the ninth-grade field trip. We had almost reached the museum complex and the end of whatever we had found to talk about. Nikisha reached into a small red purse, withdrew and opened a blue compact, and began dabbing at her face with a puffy white brush. First I looked away, embar-rassed, wondering if I was seeing something too inti-mate. Then I looked back and saw her reflection in the compact mirror. She saw mine. "Is this ridiculous?" she said. "My mother gave it to me for my birthday. Do you think I'm too young for makeup?" No, not all, I hurried to say, uneasy about having to have an opinion. She giggled, mostly at her own silliness, and also at my self-consciousness.

This self-consciousness was trivial compared to what I felt now as the fleeting memory of an ephemeral reflection of a transient existence departed.

"Hey," I said. The woman and I had reached the end of this part of the road and were turning back again. "Hey. I found some files."

I wasn't looking at my companion directly. I'm not sure that this abrupt declaration called forth from her face an expression of surprise. She had already proven to be a fast thinker, though. She would have guessed some information of significance was about to be transmitted. I thought I heard a little sound being made in the back of her throat.

I explained that while doing my inspections I had come across cartons crammed with documents relating to the conflict in the States, some of which reported incidents from our own town. I told her I didn't know how the files were brought into this country and into the enclave, but they appeared to have been dumped in the basement hurriedly, for safekeeping. The people who put them there probably still had access to the basement. They probably intended to return for them.

When I told her this, a shadow crossed her face.

"Whose files were these? Who collected the documents?"

"One of the investigative commissions," I said vaguely. "I'm not sure which."

These commissions all had similar names, with the words "justice" and "peace" and "truth" in them. When I told her the dates stamped at the top of the documents, however, she knew exactly to which commission the documents had belonged.

"Have you read them?"

"Not every one. But I saw the Target testimony. People are identified. There's some exacting detail," I said. I didn't speak about either the list of the dead or the list of the detained.

She shook her head violently. "The commission was disbanded because it was so obviously not impartial. Everyone knew that it was compromised. Look who was on it!" She named several of the international jurists, men and women widely known to have committed horrific crimes in their own countries. "Those files were supposed to have been destroyed. There was supposedly independent confirmation that they had been destroyed! The so-called evidence they collected would have been preserved for one purpose only: to go after us in the future. And that's what's happening now. We knew they were hoping to reconvene the commission, but no one knew they had the old testimony. They could have brought it here only with support from one of the native factions."

She added, "Plus someone in the police. Someone who knew where they could hide it."

I said that I didn't understand the politics, something I said regularly, to everyone, though in fact the outline of the politics was usually as discernible as a ship approaching through heavy fog, the counterpoint in a fugue, an erased pencil sketch, or the afterimage that followed a blinding snapshot flash. Almost as clear as day. I usually said I didn't understand politics in order to avoid expressing judgment. She wouldn't accept this, now that I had read the files.

"Look, Ron, a lot of bad things happened in our town. I'm not proud of what happened. But you have to understand how frightened, how terrorized everyone was—with absolutely good reason, as you will remember from before you left. Unexplained disappearances. Killings in the middle of the night. You have to understand the desperate rage too. I swear, Ron, the fear and anger were legitimate. And I know how people responded to these feelings was often wrong. It was shameful. But you can't believe everything in those files. There's another side to the story."

"What's the other side of putting people in storage cages?" I blurted, against every intention.

She flinched. It took her a moment to speak.

"Yes, the storage cages. They were terrible, one of the things I regret. But you have to know, Ron, the intention was to keep prisoners there very temporarily, like for hours. There was nowhere else to put them—and some people wanted them *killed* instead of held. So they were there for their own safety, and then the other side took the midcounty mall, so we were cut off. We had to keep them secured."

"They were beaten with braided cable wire!" I exclaimed.

She grimaced. "One or two. Is that what it says in the files? It's bullshit, Ron. It was nothing systematic. It's all lies."

"And how about the denial of medical treatment?"

"We needed that information!" she protested. "So big deal, they didn't get their Motrin until they answered a question. They bled a little. It was a matter of life or death for our people, Ron. Men, women, and children! There were real human lives at risk."

"The waterboarding."

"There was no waterboarding."

I gazed directly into her face now, studying every curve of her lips, nose, eyes, and brows, then the freckles and age marks, a few faint hairs above her lips, the traces of lipstick, the tears that welled in her eyes and magnified her pupils. I wondered how much of this I would possibly recall that night or the next year.

"Look what was happening in the Walmart on 61, next to Taco Bell," she said. "To our people. They lined up prisoners in Hardware and shot them in the head, one at a time. They held families as hostages. Joey Fleishman's mother and father. All the Satharamans. They tortured wives in front of their husbands, kids in front of their parents, parents in front of their kids. Billy Leight's grandfather. Girls as young as eleven were being raped every night. There's only one reason to rape an eleven-year-old: to ruin her life and the life of her family, for now and evermore. Teenagers were made pregnant. Kaira Satharaman was made pregnant!"

I hadn't known about Kaira, but I had heard stories like these. They were mostly credible.

Buster's wife and her dog walked away, her back turned. Now she was fully weeping, almost inaudibly, her body heaving and shuddering. Her dog watched her, gravely concerned. I felt rising up within me an impulse that solidified into an imperative to cross the distance between us. I fought it like a demon, against every element of my nature. I seized on the image of the storage cages and kept it in front of me. It kept on slipping away. I pulled it back.

The woman finally faced me again, about fifteen paces away, her face puffy, her mascara in streaks. She had stopped weeping.

She said, "I *know* the rules of war. I know the Fourth Geneva Convention: the atrocities of one side don't justify atrocities by the other. I knew that at the time. But you can ask anyone in the street in any country of the world, and certainly in any country that's at war, and they will insist that one side's acts of cruelty *do* justify ruthlessness by the other. An eye for an eye, they'll say. The other side did it first, they'll say. You have to respond with equal force, or more force, so it doesn't happen again, they'll say. They'll tell you that anywhere in the world, Ron."

I too had heard these sentiments expressed, in a variety of languages. People thought "an eye for an eye" was like some physical principle discovered by Newton.

"That's how people were thinking in America, Ron. Both sides. It's the one thing we agreed on."

SHE TURNED AGAIN AND she and her dog walked into the advancing twilight. I watched them leave, wondering if I'd ever see her again. At the end of the road, where the dusk had nearly merged the two creatures, they stopped. She came back now, her steps very deliberate. Her face was entirely composed. For a moment, though, I wasn't sure she was the same woman, especially since this woman was wearing very old black plastic-rimmed eyeglasses, which I may have seen her wear only once before, very briefly, in a mirror.

"Ron, I have to ask you this. Where are the files?"

"I can't tell you."

"Please tell me."

"I can't."

"Please."

"No."

"Please."

I told her, my resolve giving away explosively, the regret that followed overcoming me like a rush of seawater fathoms deep. The air was pounded out of my lungs. I was as weak as anyone.

"The building's locked," I said.

"You'll give me the key?"

"I'll be fired."

"You'll let me in?"

"That's impossible," I said. "No, I can't do that."

✦

We made a time to meet but I didn't promise to be there. Yet neither of us was surprised when I arrived, pedaling around the corner of the municipal building at about one thirty in the morning, my headlight dark. Nor was I surprised that the baseball-indifferent man who now called himself Buster Williams was there too, standing by two white SUVs, even if I had never considered the likelihood that his wife would tell him about the files. Of course she would tell him. Of course I couldn't now change my mind about letting them into the building, which I had crazily thought was still a possibility. The expression on her face seemed apologetic, but perhaps it wasn't.

Buster's men were with him, their postures defensive. The possibility of a double cross had fluttered their minds. Buster fiercely studied me before grasping my hand. We shook hands without saying anything, as if worried that we might be heard somewhere in the fitfully dozing enclave.

I held on to the master key. They grimly followed me through the back door and past the doors after that. The henchmen stayed close to my side, directing their flashlights down hallways and into hidden recesses, no one speaking. We descended into the storeroom and they scoured the room with their lights. The document cartons were precisely where I had left them, which was almost as great a shock as their absence would have been. The light beams collected on the boxes, making them virtually incandescent.

The married couple crouched at the cartons, their backs to us, for a tenderly private moment. They looked first at the files from our town, which remained in the carton at the top. Flipping through the other boxes, they murmured a series of familiar American place-names as if it were an incantation. A few famous individuals were named as well.

As they examined the documents, I shrank back from the center of the room. No one noticed, they were so intent on their discovery. When Buster finally stood, it took him a moment to find me in the shadows.

"You little dipshit. You dumb cocksucker," he said. He rushed over. "You came through, goddammit!"

Buster's embrace was as intimate as any I had enjoyed in years, probably since. . . . The others watched us intently, wondering what he would do next. When he pulled away, I saw that he was in tears.

"Ron, as long as I live, I'll never forget this," he

said. "You've saved many people's freedom, possibly other people's lives. You knew what to do in the moment when it needed to be done. That's what it takes sometimes, what Henry David Fucking Thoreau called a majority of one: a single person listening to his conscience. That person, he said, has more right to authority than any wrongheaded, democratically elected legislature. More right to authority than any unjust law."

"But how can he know he's right?" I objected. "Everyone thinks they're right."

He tapped his chest. "I know."

He was guided by his own moral compass, he said. He could do only what he thought was correct.

"That's what you'll tell The Hague?"

He grinned. The men had closed the boxes and had begun carrying them one at a time out of the basement, up the stairs, and through the building's unlit halls, their steps echoing.

I said, "People are aware those files were put here. They'll be looking for them."

He told me not to worry.

"They'll know I was the one who had access. They'll be looking for me. They may be the same people who burned down the Target."

"Ron, you're on the team," Buster said soberly. "You were here for us. The team is going to be here for you too. I promise you that."

"I don't need to be on a team," I protested. "I just don't want to lose my job. Or my head. Somebody went to a lot of trouble to bring these files here."

He nodded. "I know, but we'll watch your back. You have any kind of problem, we'll take care of it. A lot of bad people are running around the district, unfortunately, but we can handle them. Sometimes you have to show a little force, spend a little cash, or come up with new IDs. We're good at new IDs. Our graphic designers are the best in the business and we're completely at your service."

"That's very kind," I said, but in fact I was flooded with apprehension. Telling Buster's wife about the files was easily the most foolish thing I had ever done abroad. The compulsion had been so deeply felt that I never considered the consequences.

His wife said, "Buster, he's not political." I thought she sounded concerned.

"I know, and that's cool." Buster grinned. "Politics? It's not like we're about to get the right to vote in this fucking country. Who knows if the people here are going to keep it for themselves?"

As they were taking away the last of the cartons, she shot me a quick look weighted with a significance that I couldn't identify. It may have been a warning or perhaps it was an expression of sympathy or even, I wanted to imagine, the recollection of a previous affection. I could take my choice, which didn't mean every choice was correct. She didn't look at me again before they left.

Their boots on the stairs echoed through the basement. I listened for the ignition of the vehicles' engines. It
came and I waited a while longer, trying to settle myself.

✦

This episode in the basement of a forgotten municipal
office building in a distant, slummy neighborhood
outside the city was hardly as important as certain
concurrent national events that even the insular
English-language media were obliged to report. After
a few more twists and turns in the domestic crisis,
the fractious coalition government declared a reorga-
nization of several governmental departments. These
included the Ministry of the Interior, which oversaw
the local police agencies. The enclave's press, which
employed few journalists who had mastered our
hosts' politics (or their language), was unable to make
clear what this development meant for the migrant
population.

In the native media, I saw a few related stories about
the investigative commission, its arrival less imminent
than previously reported, if I correctly understood these
new reports, or if I had not misunderstood the original
reporting. Questions had been raised with the appropri-
ate international authorities about the scope and composition of the tribunal, how it would be funded, where
it would convene—and especially whether sufficient

evidence was available to warrant its resumption. No reporting about the commission was available in English.

WHILE I BROODED OVER these abstract uncertainties, my supervisor gave me something specific to worry about: the equipment in the former municipal building had gone dead, just a week after the cartons had been removed. She said she was surprised. The unit had transmitted none of the usual warning signals.

I quickly biked to the building, while at the same time urging myself to slow down sufficiently to think things through. The unit shouldn't have failed. If it had failed, it was because someone had made it fail. That someone very likely knew that I would be the one to fix it. I took note of every vehicle parked on the side streets. I reminded myself that I still had the pepper spray and also that it would be useless. I was only mildly relieved that the building's back door was still locked, as was every next door that I opened. I sampled the air as I walked down the long hallways, listening for human sounds or odors that could possibly be carried by it.

I unlocked the last door, hesitating before I entered. As my flashlight wanly illuminated the walls of the room, I immediately saw that the equipment panel was open, the circuit board half-pulled out. Fuck, I thought, even while I confirmed what purpose this might serve. The unit should have been disabled before the board was disconnected and I could see at once that it hadn't been, and the panel itself was damaged, probably pried open with a heavy tool. The repair would take hours.

I went to the unit, calculating the work that lay ahead. I was also aware of something, somebody, behind me. I wrapped my hand around the pepper spray canister but distracted myself by thinking out the order of the operations that were necessary to fix the unit. I would have to make sure the power was cut before I did anything. I thought of which tools I would need. There was another sound in the room. It seemed to have been made deliberately.

Eventually I turned around.

I was surprised that the sound belonged to the detective. I relaxed a little.

"Long time," I said. "I thought you were reassigned."

He said his prayers consistently went unanswered. No one had been reassigned. I shouldn't believe what I read in the papers. It didn't conform to reality. The news never did. He said, "What do you have for me?"

I thought the question was strange, as if this were one of our usual encounters. I asked him if he had pulled open the unit.

"How does it work in America?" he said, exasperated. "You interrogate the cops?"

I said that serious damage had been done to the equipment. I would have to file a report.

He wanted to know who I had seen around the enclave, especially in this neighborhood near the former municipal building. No one, really, I said. What had I heard or learned? He said there had been reports of activity inside the building. Did I know anything about it? Only that someone wrecked the equipment, I said, glaring. He asked me if there had been any signs that someone else was using the building. He asked when I had been here last.

I continued to respond vaguely or in the negative. I could see that he was annoyed.

"Some things have gone missing," he declared.

"What things?"

"I don't know. They won't tell me."

"Who won't?"

He stared for a while, trying to read me—to gauge my honesty, my sincerity, my evasiveness, whatever—but, of course, the strangeness of my American face made me inscrutable. The enclave was really a lousy assignment for a detective.

"My superiors," he confessed. "Maybe they don't know either. They don't get told everything. That's why they want me to ask you. Someone told someone to tell someone to tell me to ask you if you knew about something taken from this basement. It was important, they said."

"What can I possibly know?" I said. "I'm just a repairman."

The detective made a sigh, which in this country was expressed almost like a belch. He said, "Four beautiful students were killed. A brave soldier lost his eyesight.

This country is facing a lot of difficulties right now. Most of these have to do with us: our own complicated history, our own complicated contradictions. But now you Americans have become part of the problem. This could end with all of you being expelled. Many people already want that to happen. That's why you have to help me."

"I will," I said earnestly, but I didn't tell him anything about the removed documents.

✦

After I fixed the equipment, the company sent a team to change the locks in the building. This was normal procedure after a reported break-in.

What was odd, however, was that I was immediately given the building's new master key—which I probably wouldn't have needed to use until my next inspection. This was not likely for another year. The supervisor casually passed it to me across the counter—*too* casually, I thought—and I casually took it, not showing any kind of question in my face. She was a native; she was also a new hire, perhaps reflecting a change in the company's governance. The key was silvery bright. I fastened it to my key chain, where it seemed to take on extra weight.

✦

Very few English-language books made it into the country, where there was no market for them among the native-born people. The enclave wasn't sufficiently prosperous to support a bookstore any more than America was, but community leaders established a reading room in a high-ceilinged former creamery whose other spaces were fully inhabited. The collection comprised mostly well-traveled paperbacks discarded by the storage-starved migrants. Titles that could cause offense were declined.

I often went there on my day off, after walking the dog. Although its few books—romance novels, religious texts, novelizations of ludicrous films—were of little interest to me, I read them anyway, if only to hear words in my head that I didn't generate myself. I took pleasure in these several hours beyond the enclave's anxieties and strife.

This modest entertainment was disrupted by the arrival of Buster's wife the following Sunday. She took the chair opposite mine, scraping it against the linoleum. I raised my head, surprised. She had selected the reading room's single art book, a compilation of bathers, which she now lay on the chipped folding table without opening. The other readers in the room shortly left, apparently recognizing her as being associated with a militia. They made their departures as unobtrusively as possible.

She watched me read. Whenever I looked up, she tried to catch my eye, but I went back to my book, which I was getting through with some difficulty. After a while she opened her book and thumbed through the familiar pictures, a few of which seized her attention. Then she raised her head. She obviously wanted to speak with me, but this place was nevertheless a library.

We remained there the entire afternoon, stealthily watching each other, neither rising to use the bathroom. At closing time we brought our books back to the custodian. She accepted them silently, turning away, also uneasy about the militia's interest in the facility. Buster's wife followed me outside.

We were most of the way across the parking lot. "Ron, we need your help again," she murmured.

I smiled thinly in a way that I hoped would indicate refusal with regret, but she didn't get it. She had tried to catch my eye in the reading room. Now she was looking away, mostly at the ground.

"We need to get back into the building," she said.

These words arrested me just as I was about to reach my bicycle. I turned to survey the area. No other vehicles besides her SUV were in the parking lot, but perhaps someone was stationed in one of the low brick buildings down the street. She saw me search, but she gave no indication that we weren't being watched. We certainly were being watched, probably by someone irritated by the number of hours that we had wasted reading our books.

"There's some material we need to keep safe for a few days," she said, speaking so quietly it was a strain to hear her. I thought it may have also been a strain for her to speak. Her voice wavered as she explained, "A few boxes. Nothing much. I wouldn't ask you if it wasn't important. It'll take us just fifteen minutes to drop it off."

"I can't get in," I said. The new silvery key tugged at my belt. It felt like it was about to fly off. "They've changed the locks."

✦

Again I woke in the middle of the night and had to convince my dog that she wasn't invited to come. I padded through the former printing plant past huddled families and double-concaved couples. A few sleepers stirred and I whispered that they shouldn't worry, it was only me, though not everyone knew who I was and how little or how much I should worry them. I put on my boots once I stepped outside the building. I sat on a rock for a while.

No one was waiting when I eventually glided into the lot at the back of the former municipal offices. Perhaps Buster's plans had changed, I hoped. I biked once around the building. I continued to hope that I could return home, but then the faint distant roar of approaching vehicles became perceptible. They were coming from a far distance at a high velocity. I also knew they numbered several more than the two SUVs that were here last time.

They swept around the building in close formation,

their lights off, three or four SUVs, followed by several flatbed pickups. For a moment I thought I was about to be run over in the dark, but the lead vehicle stopped short. The passenger door swung open and Buster jumped out before the last truck shut its engine. The SUVs emptied. One of the men with Buster started giving orders. He was unusually tall. Tailgates dropped. Tarps were being removed from the backs of the trucks.

Buster rushed at me. He cried, "You stupid mother-fucker!"

I half hid in his grip, wondering what to make of the tall militiaman's presence. The last time I had seen him he had been setting fire to the memorial erected by Buster's militia.

A woman finally emerged from the last SUV, her head down. I watched her from over Buster's shoulder. She tentatively stayed near her vehicle, as if she had just wandered onto the scene. She seemed a little dazed, a little disheveled. I thought, perhaps without cause, that she had recently been struck.

Now the tall militiaman saw me and gradually seemed to recognize me—possibly as the guy whose dog had taken a dump in the empty lot. He would have seen me around elsewhere too. Everyone had. He stared to make sure that I knew he had identified me. He didn't trust me and I wondered how much he trusted Buster.

Buster impatiently watched as I fumbled with the new locks at the building's back door. I opened the next door

and the one after that down the stairs, the tall militiaman
and the other men following on our heels. We never, however, reached the room with the equipment I had repaired.
A high cavernous space sprawled off the basement hallway. Buster had seen the doorless former boiler room the
first time he was here. The men behind him brought in a
bank of battery-operated high-intensity lamps, their glare
harsh and unevenly distributed, deepening the shadows
in the parts of the room they didn't reach. The remains of
the furnace glowed as if fired up again.

It took two and three men to carry down the stairs
and into the room each of the wooden crates that were
being delivered. They were much larger and heavier
than the cardboard cartons that had been removed
the previous week. I had been expecting cardboard. I
walked away to stand in the room's unlit distant corner.
Buster's wife came in, not looking at the boxes, and she
also disappeared into the dark. With the tall militiaman
supervising, crates of different sizes were being neatly
stacked along the far wall.

Buster called across the room: "Ronnie, where are
you? I have to show you something!"

"That's OK, thanks! I don't want to get in the way."

"Don't be an asshole," he said. "You've got to see
these babies."

I came over reluctantly. I was indeed in the way as
another case was brought in. Breathing hard, the men
awkwardly stepped around me. Buster grinned. He had

opened one of the deeper crates and removed a maroon carton about nine inches long. He removed the cover to reveal a knobby, cylindrical device resting on a bed of soft white cotton.

"German," he said. "Not under sanctions and totally legal, technically. Top-of-the-line tactical."

I knew what it was. He touched the night vision switch and handed it to me.

The gunsight was far more sophisticated than the hunting scopes I had used as a kid, cool to the touch and highly styled. I raised it to my eye.

The room was entirely lit now, cast in a green luminescence, its walls brought close. The walls' fine-grain texture was expressed in every different kind of green. The basement's hidden debris, its rags, small tools, and old paint cans, were turned into jewels, specifically emeralds. They had been left here before the Americans came.

I swung the field of view across the depths of the basement and again I was visited by the sensation of standing in a spinning room. The room stopped abruptly when I reached the green, burning face of Buster's wife, invisible to anyone else but now pinned by my crosshairs. The vertigo remained. She raised her head and gazed directly at me. My eyes met hers. Something rippled across her face.

Buster said, "Pretty amazing, huh? We have three hundred of them."

I returned the tactical sight to my face and again I

studied his wife, as I had many times before, through one apparatus or another. Her glowing eyes found mine again. The years collapsed on themselves.

I handed back the device. Buster was called away by one of his men. The man was studying some papers attached to a locally made clipboard, which was constructed along lines very different from the clipboards with which Americans were familiar.

I followed Buster along the wall and we reached a section of much larger crates, which were still being stacked. Some of these boxes were longer and shallower than the ones that contained the optical equipment. Others were simply square. Both kinds of crates were stamped with the words *PRODUCT OF USA*, the first time I had seen that phrase in years.

I stooped to read what else was written on the crates. One of the words was immediately recognizable.

I said, "Soybeans?"

Buster put his hands on the backs of my shoulders, massaging them. "Yeah, soybeans," he confirmed. "Six tons of soybeans, buddy-boy!"

The tall militiaman approached, scowling at Buster for bringing me to this part of the room. He was also on the verge of recognizing that I might have had something to do with the removal of the files. We turned and walked back, Buster still chuckling.

We passed through the glare produced by the high-intensity lamps. I covered my eyes and realized that a few minutes earlier, when Buster gave me the gunsight, I may have been standing in the dark, not visible from the other unlit places in the basement. I wasn't sure now where I had stood. I could reasonably wonder whether Buster's wife had seen me when I put the scope to my face.

The men completed stacking the crates and filed out. The lamps were turned off but were left in the room. I locked every door as Buster, his wife, the tall militiaman, and I went back the way we came, none of us speaking. Once we were outside, I relocked the chains on the door. The tall militiaman tested them. Without being asked I knew to give him the key.

✦

Only a few hours were left before morning, but I returned to the printing plant and lay on my cot, a hand dropped into the fur of the animal resting more successfully on the little throw rug that had been salvaged from somewhere. The crates that I had seen in the boiler room of the former municipal building were now part of my life—and I would pretend that I hadn't seen them, just as I would resume my pretension that I hadn't seen the files taken from another part of the basement. I knew how to pretend not to see things.

I must have dozed for a bit, without dreaming, gradually half waking to the awareness that someone was sitting in a bridge chair pulled up to my bedside. It was a man, a native, probably the detective. He was smoking. With my eyelids almost fully lowered, I thought how unusual it was for a native-born person to enter on his own a building inhabited by Americans, allowing himself to be surrounded by Americans. I thought dimly how uncomfortable this man must be and, therefore, how urgent his business was. I may have dropped off again for a moment.

When I came to, I was aware that I had been asked about what had happened in the basement of the municipal building that night. I may have already begun mumbling about the agricultural commodities that were among America's few legal exports. I didn't speak of the tall militiaman or anyone else, but I suggested the possibility that we were fundamentally mistaken about which forces were arrayed against each other and why. We might be mistaken, too, about the structures of society embedded into past and current history. But I thought there would be tremendous bloodshed and loss of life in the enclave. These were probably very advanced agricultural commodities.

The detective may have muttered something contemptuous about the fucking Americans, though I couldn't tell whether it related to the militias or to the people occupying the printing plant and now pretending to sleep. It may have been something to the effect that for all he cared we could kill ourselves off. But he said he would alert his superiors. This was their problem, not his.

I must have fallen asleep again and I didn't see him leave. When I finally woke, the bridge chair was returned to its usual place. None of my cohabitants made a remark about the predawn visitation, nor about the tobacco-like smoke that lingered in the rough, makeshift dwelling space, where the no-smoking injunctions were enforced more rigorously than any other communal mandate, but it seemed that they made an effort not to look in my direction. I imagined that the former printing plant was now infected by another strain of fear and suspicion. I would have to find a new place to live. One of the containers perhaps.

THERE WAS NOTHING FOR me to do that morning but go to work. Even though I had a full call sheet, I went out of my way to bike past the former municipal building, staying out of sight but hoping to see police activity. The parking lot around the building remained empty throughout the afternoon.

As the day was ending, I returned to the plant for my dog. We again walked along the creek and a woman was there, standing still, her back to me. Even her dog was facing away. I assumed they would turn as we approached. They didn't. I could have headed in the other direction before her dog barked and she saw me. I didn't.

When I reached her she didn't say hello or acknowledge that I had joined her. Neither did her dog. We walked side by side, parallel to the creek.

At the end of the road we turned. My dog pulled on the leash, wanting to go ahead. I pulled back and very deliberately pronounced the dog's name, as the woman might have expected me to.

Now she asked me about the city that shared my dog's name. Was it a pleasant place to live? I told her my life there had been difficult, but the city itself contained many charms and surprises. I spoke about the shrine to the poets on the rock to the north of the city, the miniature-golf resort complex to the south, the inhabitants' simultaneously wise and silly sayings, the faint and mournful throat singing that you might hear at the close of day without knowing from where it was coming, and the annual lovers' festival that celebrated the ascension of the planet Venus to its highest point in the morning sky. I excavated from the past as many artifacts as I could. I had been saving them for her all this time.

She wanted to know about the work I did there. I explained how it was similar to the maintenance job I held now, but that the equipment was usually situated on the roofs of buildings, whether they were residential or commercial. I enjoyed that part of the job. I told her how I appreciated the city from its high places, which offered magnificent views of the bay. I explained how the city's housing shortage, like the shortage in the enclave, had required people to make ingenious residential use of the roofs, either in shanties or other makeshift dwellings, some of them cut out of existing apartments. I had to move among these structures to find my equipment, I said.

"I suppose you could have looked in people's windows."

I made myself laugh. "What do you mean?"

"I don't know. Spied on them, I guess, if they couldn't see you."

"I wouldn't do that," I declared.

She said, "Weren't you curious? Didn't you want to see how people lived? What they had on their walls? What kind of kitchen appliances they used? Whether they were tidy or sloppy? What if there was a woman coming out of the shower? Wouldn't you have at least watched her?"

"What do you think I am, a Peeping Tom?" This exchange was accomplished only with great effort on my part. There was nothing teasing in the woman's manner. She was grimly deliberate in constructing a narrative or, rather, in settling our accounts. She wanted me to see her plainly for whom she had always been. My dog made little mewling sounds, as if she knew that I was upset. "No," I emphasized, resisting the transparent. "I never watched anybody."

In the city where she herself had temporarily settled, she said, the international investigative commission had found her and issued a summons. She would have had to give testimony. They already had certain damaging information in their possession, she conceded. She reminded me that the commission was partisan, composed of some of the most criminal characters from some of the most criminal countries, but the local authorities were cooperating at the time. They would have compelled her to testify, even against herself.

Then the cooperation ended and the commission departed, but she knew other investigators would come looking for her. The warrants were still out there. She immediately changed flats and found a new job. She had to obtain new papers.

She said, "It required some tremendous string pulling in a city where no one knew me or could possibly know me. So it required concessions and compromises and actions on my part that were particularly degrading. But after what happened in America I thought my life couldn't be degraded further. Or I thought I deserved any degradation that came my way."

It took her a long time, she added, longer than it should have, to realize that she was engaged in a struggle to survive—not as a woman with a basic quality of life or as an independent woman or a decent woman or a woman whose personal identity was intact, but rather as a simple living organism.

To survive, she had to think of herself as another person, from another country, with another history. Every thought of America was a dangerous lapse.

"I've made concessions too," I said quietly.

She continued, "And then when I needed to come to this country other papers were necessary. New documentation was made for me. I had to think of myself as a third woman, this time as another American. That other woman: this is who I am now."

It was getting dark. I could no longer see her face easily. Our dogs had both stopped for a moment to look into the still water near where the creek met the road. They either looked at their own reflections or at each other's.

I told her that my own concessions meant working with the police. I had been doing it for months. I wasn't much of an informer, I said. The cops never used my information. But they were interested in the militias. They possibly already knew about last night's delivery to the former municipal building. I had been obligated to tell them, though, in fact, I conceded, I wasn't sure that I really had.

It took her a few moments to move away from the recollection of what she had done to reach the enclave, to recall what she had given up. The implications of what I was saying now descended upon her only gradually, like a soaking mist. Eventually, she spoke. "Just terrific. Buster's not going to be happy. Depending on the cops. Which cops did you tell?"

"Just one detective, some guy with a weird native name. He's been my contact."

"Do you know who he's reporting to?"

I couldn't answer that. She didn't seem especially shocked or disgusted by my collaboration, or by my uncertainty. She shook her head, her anger directed elsewhere. "Buster's such an idiot, always looking for trouble. I tried to stop this. I fought him every way I could. I'm sorry I had to get you involved, but he forced me. Look, it's just a transshipment issue. I'll make sure the material's gone tonight. I promise."

"And then what?" I protested. "More violence? Enough Americans aren't being killed in America? We have to start killing each other here?"

She frowned severely. "I swear, I hope not. That's not the plan."

"These are dangerous gangs," I said. "They've terrorized every decent American in the district. It's not hard to imagine what they'll do with high-powered weapons. They're at constant war with each other. The tall militiaman burned down half a block of homes! How can you even be involved with him?"

It took her a moment to figure out whom I was talking about. "Another idiot. Two bipartisan idiots. They think they're business partners now that the commission's dead. Actually, they think they're statesmen. Begin and Sadat. Mandela and de Klerk. They're going to bring the district peace and prosperity. When you hear Buster talk, you can almost believe him, or fully believe him, but out here, with you, in the dark, I swear to God, I don't."

I said, "Do you still have the red passport? The passport from the other country?"

She didn't speak for a while. Our dogs pulled on

their leashes, trying to take us away from this particular place in the road.

"I do," she finally admitted, coming close. Her eyes captured some stray light from elsewhere, possibly from another city. "It's buried in my underwear drawer. I look at it from time to time."

I asked if the passport was still valid. She didn't answer, which I took as an affirmative.

"Then come with me," I proposed. I told her that we had to get out of the enclave. I told her about the hamlet that I had visited in the northern province. The people there were kind and hospitable, I promised. My friends would protect us. We would live with them, learn their customs, get local jobs, and learn the language. We would learn the language so well that we would speak it between ourselves. We would think like natives. If she was carrying the other passport, no one would ever find her.

"I can't do that," she said, not remarking on my plan's absolute impracticality. For one thing, I myself didn't have alternative papers. I would have been findable almost immediately.

"You *can* do that," I insisted.

"I can't."

"Please," I begged.

"I'm sorry, Ron."

"Please."

"I can't leave Buster."

"But," I said.

"He's still the father of my son."

"But your son is . . ." I said.

I couldn't possibly finish the sentence, with all its logical, fatal obviousness.

After their boy was taken away all they had left was their memory of him, she said. That's what they had carried away from America. There were certain details of the boy's existence—a toy, a joke, his giggle, the way he cried when he lost his pacifier, a misconception about something he saw on TV, another misconception about the workings of the universe—that she and the boy's father now kept between them, trading these particulars back and forth in the dark across their bed in the middle of the night.

"There are things about him that only I remember, Ron, things I can tell his father. Some things only his father remembers. There'll be some kind of settlement in America someday, maybe an amnesty, and we'll go back. We'll find him and tell him what we remember. He's a young man now. We'll be able to tell him who he is."

I couldn't remind her of how the administrative records had been poorly kept, scattered, and lost. I couldn't remind her of the deadly violence that had been committed against children and young adults.

Instead I said, "Come with me and you'll tell me the stories, all the stories. Everything you remember. He'll become as tangible and substantial and real to me as he is to you."

"Like an image in a mirror," she said sadly. One of our dogs made a little sound. "OK, I'll come."

I must have lost track of her in the gloaming, because I never saw her close in as she placed her lips against mine. Her eyes were shut. I shut mine. All we had for a while were our lips and the heat of our embrace. There was nothing tentative or ambiguous or unknown about the kiss. We knew what it meant. We knew the city from where it originated.

As we drew apart, I said, "You will?"

"No, that's impossible."

"But you just said you'll come!"

"I can't. Buster and I are going to find him someday."

"There won't be a settlement," I said, but I can't be sure now whether I said this with sympathetic warmth or with the most bitter, coldest cruelty. "We'll never be able to go back to America."

The woman left me then, her shape and her dog's shape dissolving into the other gray forms that bubbled within and near the creek. There were hardly any working streetlights in this part of the enclave. My dog barked once in farewell.

ON THE WAY BACK to the former printing plant, I tried to explain to my dog what Buster's wife had said about the two militias. I added that I couldn't do anything about them. I reminded her that I had survived this long by staying out of politics. But I couldn't explain what the militias might do with their weapons, what the guns might mean for the ordinary unarmed Americans in the district also trying to stay out of politics. I couldn't convince her that I didn't care.

I made sure she had enough water for the night. Then I biked to the neighborhood where the former municipal building was located, taking the backstreets. I quickly passed the building, which was still chained tight, unattended by any legal authority that could save us from ourselves.

There was a former indigenous religious tower a few blocks away. The medieval stone edifice was several stories high, all winding staircases and curved walls, unexpected lookouts and turrets, garishly ornamented with colored glass and variously shaped mirrors, as was the custom in this country. American migrants fully occupied the structure, their families showing admirable originality and persistence in making living spaces out of the shrine's alcoves, chapels, and passageways.

I had worked in the tower's damp basement only a month earlier, but the occupants knew me and didn't question why I needed to climb to the top of the building, where there was no equipment to inspect. So much about life as a migrant was strange anyway. I waved my toolbox as I passed their rooms and some of the Americans waved back. The family on the top floor was pleased to see me, almost as if I was expected. Their little girl looked up from the kitchen table to show me a drawing of something. I went out to the tower's circular parapet.

The air was still warm and the darkness in the enclave was complete, save for the occasional house lights that randomly spotted the continuum. I wouldn't be seen, not from this distance, but to be sure I positioned myself on the other side of the tower. A piece of broken concave reflective glass was fastened to the ceiling of the tiled overhang. The magnified image of the enclave rotated across the glass as I approached. Once I properly positioned myself, I could observe the rear of the former municipal building.

The child came out to the parapet to show me another drawing or perhaps it was the same drawing. I studied it again. It was no better than any other four-year-old's sketch: a series of stick figures. They represented other children, I supposed, her friends or the friends she someday hoped to have. Their smiles were as wide as their faces. Her mother came out to carry her off to bed. The girl wanted me to keep the sketch, which I folded neatly and deposited in my toolbox.

As the family quieted down for the night, so did the enclave, which then, in slumber, seemed enormous, larger than the country hosting us, as oversized as our American dreams had always been. The district stretched to every horizon. I felt an anxious affection for the place and for its inhabitants. The stars brightened. Their constellations were unfamiliar to us, constructed from illusions and myths that belonged to another people.

Hours later the trucks arrived, again without headlights. They may have not been the same trucks. From my perch, even with its magnifying mirror, I couldn't see the men getting out, but I may have heard the creaking whine of the building's metal outer door as it opened, the sound carried tremulously in the barely perceptible breeze. The men themselves couldn't be heard. After a while a glow from the battery-operated lamps in the basement mounted the steps and radiated from the open door.

I looked for her, but the woman hadn't come tonight. I had thought I might see her one more time. I could now recognize Buster and the tall militiaman. They were standing to the side, watching the trucks being loaded. The men didn't seem to need direction from them. Staring hard at the shard of glass, I was jolted by the realization that the men and the drivers of the trucks were natives. I could tell from their body and head shapes, their postures, their skin pigmentation, their clothes, and their deportment. It was exceedingly odd, almost impossible, to see them in the enclave so late at night, and also in the company of American criminals.

I waited. At any time, I thought, the detective might yet join me, arriving soundlessly, and we would observe the disposition of the gunsights and the soybeans together. From my place I had a good view of the enclave's nearby neighborhoods, which were jam-packed with the dreaming adherents of one theory of reality or another. Now the trucks were being loaded and their scarlet taillights snaked out of the parking lot in pairs. I remained alone.

I shifted my place so that I could better watch the course they were taking, but I lost the convoy. Several anxious moments passed before I could find the correct vantage point. They weren't heading down one of the main streets into the populated neighborhoods of the enclave. As it exited the parking lot, the lead vehicle had turned left and the others followed.

From where I watched, I couldn't see them reach the coastal road, but there was nowhere else the trucks could have gone.

✦

I didn't return to the former printing plant. Once I left the tower, stepping past the mostly still bodies of my fellow migrants, I went for what might have appeared to be a recreational nighttime bike ride, not that anyone in the district ever did that. I glided down one street after another, easily visible to anyone who was looking for me. I wanted it to be the detective. I stopped at a few places, whistling to myself. Here I am. Here I am. No one was looking for me. I sensed, for the first time in months, that I was no longer under surveillance. This made me feel more lonely than before, as lonely as anyone on a planet where conscience was a human construction.

I checked my watch. The hours of the night were inexorable and so was the passage of the soybean-laden trucks on the two-lane road going north. I wondered if she was sleeping now. I knew how she slept: usually on her back, her lips parted and chapped, her left hand often half-raised to her face.

Dawn arrived stealthily, with just a grayish lightening of the sky, so that I couldn't identify the moment when night actually ended. I waited, reminding myself that I could forget what I had witnessed being taken from the municipal building. I experimented with forgetting what I had witnessed. I experimented with having no idea what it meant. The day's early car traffic began to fill the road and a few shopkeepers raised their grilles.

Then the first clump of children began to coagulate at a school bus stop, some half-asleep, some in animated conversation. They ignored me too. At this hour children in every province would be waiting for their school buses, which in this country were weirdly painted a bright teal blue. There was another stop with more kids. I locked my bike to a sign pole in front of the enclave's single police station.

It was an imposing ancient structure, dating from another century and a time before anyone in this country had ever heard of Americans. The building's grimy gray stone was crumbling and every window was too filthy to reveal what was behind it. In recent years, as the enclave was increasingly taken over by migrants, the government had lost all interest in its upkeep.

I went through the open doors into a short, dim corridor that led to a booth that was clouded by scratched glass. The man behind the heavy glass, someone analogous to a desk sergeant, stared at me with a crooked, humorless smile that in this country expressed incredulity. Very few Americans entered the facility under their own power.

Using the local language, I asked to speak with my detective. I carefully pronounced what I remembered of his name. When nothing like recognition showed on the sergeant's face, I repeated the name, as best as I could, and then I repeated it again.

He asked finally, in his language, "What do you want?"

I said the detective's name again. I told the sergeant that the situation was urgent. Perhaps I used a word that was similar to urgent, but didn't carry precisely the same meaning. With some impatience, the sergeant pointed to a bench and told me to wait. He went back to whatever he was doing. I sat and I saw cops come in, wearing their distinctive pink uniforms, as well as men and women who I presumed were plainclothes detectives. A few glanced at me with indifference. All of them looked familiar. The sergeant didn't appear to call anyone. After about a half hour I returned to the window. The sergeant gazed at me as if he had never seen me before. Again he asked me what I wanted. I told him the name of my detective and said it was a matter of life or death.

He again directed me to wait on the bench. I knew that I could simply leave the station house and no one would remember that I had been there. The morning stretched on. The contraband was approaching its destination. My dog would soon need to be fed and walked.

I had nearly given up and had perhaps dozed off when I was approached by a man in a suit.

"Do you need help?" he said.

"You speak English!"

He chuckled warmly. "A bit. Two of my grandparents were Guyanese."

Nothing about him looked Guyanese, but his smile was friendly. Speaking a little quickly perhaps, I told him that I knew one of their detectives. I had some very important information for him that had to be acted upon at once. The man listened patiently as I struggled to repeat my detective's name. He grinned helplessly, also not recognizing the name, and said that he was only an interpreter. He would find somebody with whom I could speak.

He brought me to a small conference room with a bridge table and chairs and asked if I would like a cup of the indigenous hot caffeinated drink. I declined, reminding him that every minute counted. He left but didn't shut the door all the way, perhaps not inadvertently. I could leave anytime, the inch of space between the door and its frame suggested. Save for a map of the district, a mirror, and a photograph of the minister of the interior, the room's walls were bare under lurid fluorescent lights. The carpeting was worn and long unacquainted with a vacuum cleaner.

The door eventually opened again and the interpreter arrived with a detective, no one I had ever seen before, I thought. The man already seemed annoyed, as if wakened from the most beautiful nap. He barely looked in my direction, but he spent a long time studying my identity papers. He took no notes. When he finally trained his eyes on me, he said in his own language, "What does he want?"

I told the interpreter that a shipment of American weapons had been smuggled into the enclave and sent by truck to the northern province early this morning. I told him how the guns had been brought in as soybeans and stored in the former municipal services building. The gunsights were top-of-the-line, I said.

The cold impassivity of the interpreter's gaze made me catch a long breath.

Then I told him who was involved, spelling out their names. Then I spelled out the names to which they had been attached in America. I added that two American criminal organizations were collaborating with each other and evidently with native persons too. I repeated that I had seen the trucks leave for the coastal road.

I stopped to let him translate.

"You know, he's like most Americans," the interpreter said. "Very emotional."

The detective grunted in acknowledgment.

I couldn't follow everything the interpreter told him. The language he used was complicated, there were digressions, and he mentioned situations and localities with which I wasn't familiar. He went on at some length. I understood, however, that he wasn't telling the detective about the weapons.

I wanted to protest that I wasn't like most Americans, that I wasn't emotional, but I held back. I was only slowly realizing that I might not want to indicate how much of the local language I had learned.

The detective asked the interpreter something that was unintelligible to me. The interpreter asked me who I had already told about the soybeans. I said I hadn't told anyone, just them. The interpreter expressed something to the detective, not about the soybeans. The detective continued his line of questioning. The interpreter asked me if I had disclosed the whereabouts of certain foreign documents to other police officials. I said I didn't know what he was talking about. He asked me directly for which side I was working. I said no side. He made a gesture of disbelief. But he told the detective that I barely made sense; again, he said, I was like most of the migrants he encountered.

The detective was getting increasingly frustrated.

Through the interpreter, he angrily asked me to repeat the story. I did, trying to be articulate, employing simple English words in declarative sentences to make them as clear as possible to the interpreter. Again I repeated the names, trying to keep my voice from wavering. I thought my manner was brisk and businesslike. I was especially careful to avoid any kind of histrionics, even as I warned of the effectiveness of contemporary weapons equipped with tactical sights, especially against poorly armed troops, even as I warned of the northern province's political volatility.

While the interpreter spoke to the detective, I gazed upon the fierce portrait of the interior minister. She was said to be in line for the prime minister's job, if one thing or another happened, though I wasn't sure what those things were or whether they had anything to do with the convoy moving north. I continued to inspect the room. I wondered how many migrants had been brought here before me. I realized then that the mirror on the wall was surely half-silvered, with no backing on the other side, which would be set in the wall of an unlit room. These devices were often called one-way mirrors or, contradictorily, two-way mirrors. Mr. Strauss had shown us how they worked.

I mostly couldn't understand what the interpreter was saying, though the story sounded familiar, if not in the sense that it bore any relation to what I had just testified. I was stunned. The tale that was evidently being

ascribed to me was preposterous, cheesy, cynical, bor-
ing, false to human emotion, and a traitor to every narrative principle.

The detective said, "It sounds like the movie!"

"It does!" the interpreter agreed. "I love that movie."

"Me too, it's great, maybe the greatest film ever
made. But why did this guy come in to tell us about it?"

They both turned to stare. I didn't dare scowl at the
interpreter. Instead I just looked across the room, pretending total incomprehension. I saw my face in the mirror,
an image of futility. This, however, was no pretension, no
exaggeration. I thought, too, that I saw something move
behind my reflection, like an angel or an imp.

"Fucking Americans," the detective said. "Always
thinking of new ways to waste our time."

"The world's time. Sorry, he said the matter was
'needful.' We thought he meant 'urgent.'"

After the detective left, still swearing, the interpreter
led me from the room. His demeanor was transformed.
He was obviously angry, but he was also unsettled and
anxious. He seized me by the elbow as he directed me
to the building's exit, in what seemed like a hurry. We
passed through a central hallway that was churning with
officers and plainclothesmen. A new shift was coming on.

"Thank you very much," the interpreter said in
English. "That was very helpful. We've already notified
the authorities in the northern province. They'll inter-
cept the weapons."

"I'm glad," I said. We approached a wall-mounted flat-screen TV. The news was on, as always. The political crisis was continuing. Officers and staff assembled below the screen and watched openmouthed. I added, "I wouldn't want there to be more violence. I like this country."

He blurted, "You don't know shit about this country."

Cops and police officials were still streaming into the building. The more intensely I stared at them, the more their features ran together.

Yet I was the single American, immediately identifiable as such, an object of mild curiosity. The arriving staff entered the building and flicked glances at me in quick succession. The interpreter kept his grip as they jostled us. Then our progress was briefly halted by a clot of men in suits and then, when we found ourselves face to face, one of the natives lingered there.

For a half moment we were each half-sure we recognized the other, but then the half moment went by and I was out of the building, on the station's front steps. As the interpreter released me, he gave me a hard push.

He said, "You goddamn American *loolie*. You should never have shown your face."

I knew the slang word from my year at sea. We had a perpetually angry Guyanese stevedore. It meant "prick."

And then I was out on the street, where my bicycle was waiting. I removed from my pocket the key to the lock. I was now alone and it was still morning. I looked around, smiling in a friendly way at the passersby, most of them migrants, most on the way to their jobs. It was an ordinary morning in the enclave. My dog had to be walked and I had to get to work. Someone ducked behind a building on the corner. His head was held at an unusually high altitude.

I kept my bike where it was. I stepped quickly to the subway entrance in front of the station house. A train was arriving, its brakes squealing. I took the stairs two at a time.

✦

The ride into the city occupied an hour in which I felt myself to be especially conspicuous, even though most of the passengers who had boarded were other Americans. One or two seemed to be watching me and one or two seemed to be taking pains not to watch me. I knew I could have been followed on the train. The morning's earlier minutes of inattention had swiftly passed.

The subway stopped at the central station on its way across the city. I remained on the train until the final moment, abruptly squeezing past the doors as they closed. I knew the station well, with long experience navigating its labyrinth of halls, escalators, food courts, and stairwells. I pursued an indirect path through the station and exited on a small backstreet.

Even on this quiet byway, though, nearly every building

surface was mirrored and in seeing myself I was reminded that I could also be watched by the ubiquitous yet hidden surveillance devices. I moved quickly, trying to outrun my reflection, which hurtled in all directions across pieces of reflective glass, a multiplicity of middle-aged American men, all of them having been in fitful motion for most of their lives.

Going down some alleyways and beneath a highway overpass sheathed in polished aluminum, I headed for the skyscraper where I had paid a service call several months earlier. I slipped through the back entrance, waving my toolbox at the half-dozing guard. I had the elevator access code.

The acceleration nearly buckled my knees. My ears popped. I thought I might have detected a slight relaxation in the earth's gravitational bonds. When the elevator door finally slid open, I took a deep breath. I stepped under a marbled sky into a moderate wind that tasted of the ocean. The vistas were as grand as ever, most of the region visible, the enclave no more than another contested patch of American dirt. I couldn't see where the district ended nor where the adjacent administrative units began, nor the next country over. There were no borders, every astronaut fallaciously observed after being sent aloft at great expense and effort by the political entity defined by its borders. No, there were borders all right, limits set by walls and fences, drones and cameras. Again, I wondered where

I could go, which new place would have me. As I gazed upon the continent, I thought I could see, snug within this country's own borders, the northern province's faraway coast.

Still thinking things through, I crossed the roof to the equipment panel. I opened my toolbox and saw the drawing the young American girl had given me last night. The stick figures depicted what may have been little children, perhaps huddled together under a smiling sun, in front of what was either a very crude attempt at a conventional American house or a slightly more accurate representation of a home that was radically strange, like the indigenous private residences in the countryside. I checked the equipment. It was working normally and wouldn't need reinspection for another year, by whoever would be doing my job then. I wrote out a brief technical note on the local version of a Post-it and stuck it inside the panel door.

I enjoyed the illusion of a clear thought. I would reach the northern province on my own by way of regional trains and commuter buses. Of course, I would be the only American among the travelers, but I would exert every one of my powers of inconspicuousness not to provoke interest, especially from the police. My papers were still valid. I could reach the hamlet within a day or two. I would throw myself upon the mercies of the warmhearted people who had already welcomed me. The old man was just crazy enough to take me in. His young niece was just bold enough to keep me protected. This is what I had promised Buster's wife and the notion had become no more fantastic and no less.

I now brought back to memory the family's house in every detail and I could see myself moving through each of the rooms they had shown me. I would wear indigenous dress and speak the indigenous language, if not fluently. I could almost hear the conversations I would have. I'd help out in the kitchen. I would fully immerse myself in the life of the family and in the work of the hamlet. I would stop running, I would no longer be a migrant. I would no longer be an American.

I now recalled the weapons and how they would be employed, either in the hamlet or nearby.

I stepped away from the panel and again gazed into the distance, perhaps hundreds of miles. A storm may have been gathering out at sea, which was dotted with tiny container ships that rose and fell among the wave crests. It was then that I became aware of the clicks and shudders of an ascending elevator car, the hum amplifying as it approached. I turned to face the door, which was at the far end of the roof. There was nothing I could do but wait.

Several long seconds passed before the door hissed open. The figure that finally jumped from it, nearly out of breath, was female.

"Ron Patterson!" she cried. She rushed across the roof. "We can't stay here. C'mon, let's go."

"How did you find me?"

"There are cameras everywhere. Also security equipment. We have access to some of it."

"You do?" I said, surprised. "You and Buster have
access to the equipment?"

Now it was her turn to be puzzled.

"What do you mean?" she said. "Buster Williams?"

I nodded. "The man you can't leave."

Now she was fully incredulous. She took a step
back, as if to get a better look at me. She was holding a
medium-size envelope.

She said, "I don't understand."

"Your husband."

"You think I'm Buster Williams's wife?" Disgust
mutilated her face, making it even less recognizable.
"Nikisha Jones? That gangster? That war criminal? I
don't look anything like her. That's not her real name
anyway."

I said, "I know."

She said hurriedly, "Buster Williams isn't his real
name either. But the international commission will eventually find them both, whatever they call themselves.
They can't escape justice forever."

She began talking quickly, still apparently rattled
by my apparent mistake. She said she belonged to an
organization that was working to bring real peace to the
district. Her name was Juliana, though when I asked if
that was her real name she frowned and didn't respond

directly. She explained that her group had supported the removal of the Target site. The shrine had dishonored the memory of the militia's many victims, though her group didn't necessarily approve the means by which the demolition had been effected, nor would her group defend the people who did it. They had blood on their hands too. The important thing, she said, was to find a new way forward for the district's Americans, for all Americans, abroad and at home. Her colleagues were impressed by the bold statement I made by walking my dog on the empty lot. They were especially stirred by the poop.

"It was inadvertent."

"That's what I said," she conceded. "But this morning you went to the police. That was brave: you were standing up against both militias and their criminal native allies. Now we know you're a hero."

"But the police ignored me!"

"No one ignored you," she said, looking at me directly. "Right now you're the least ignored American in the country. People from the government are looking for you. The opposition is looking for you. Buster Williams and his new partner are *really* looking for you."

"His partner? You mean the tall militiaman?"

"Yes, Shorty Velasquez. Another thug. They're displeased that you went to the police. I may have beat them by fifteen minutes. So we have to go right now."

"The police stopped the trucks?"

Juliana shook her head, frustrated with having to explain the obvious. She said it wasn't important whether the trucks were stopped, or at least whether these specific trucks were stopped. The trucks were only a single element in a complicated political confrontation. Sides were being taken now. I was on *her* side, no matter what, and she would get me safely out of the country.

"I have to go back for my dog," I said.

"Buster killed your dog."

Now I was the one who took a step back, recoiling in shock, and then I took another. I wasn't too far from the edge of the roof.

"I told you he was displeased," she said. "He has anger issues, I think."

"But my dog was an innocent creature!"

"Exactly," she said. "Think what he'll do to you."

At that moment, even knowing the horrors for which the man who called himself Buster Williams was responsible at our town's Target, even knowing the violence he had perpetrated in the enclave, some of it perhaps against his own wife, and even having observed his excitability, I didn't believe he was capable of hurting my dog. She was a very sweet dog. The woman may have been lying about the dog. In that case what else was she lying about?

"Here," she said, handing me an envelope.

Inside the envelope was a plane ticket and a stapled, royally emblazoned, deep-navy booklet.

"Canada?"

She told me my new name, spelling it out. That's who I would be from this moment forward. There was a place for me in Toronto. She added, "Don't think this was easy or cheap, or that it was done with the, uh, full support of my organization. Don't be so sure it's foolproof either. You'll find out at passport control."

"Come with me," I said.

"I'm not who you think I am. I'm not Nikisha Jones," she insisted. "I'm the mirror-opposite of Nikisha Jones."

"Come with me anyway."

She pretended to laugh. It was a very weak pretension. There may have been something wet in her eyes. "I'm not Amanda Keller either."

"Come. We'll both have new identities. New lives, with new, better stories to tell each other. We'll make a real future, with a new family. We'll watch hockey. It's really a fun game if you can follow the puck. Please, come with me. Marlise, you have to."

Her head turned so that I couldn't see her face, she hurried me to the elevator. I tried to speak with her as we made the stomach-churning drop, which seemed to cover a much greater distance than the ascent. I dug through my archives. I wanted to tell her about the sweet breakfast roll that was popular in the city on the bay. I wanted to mention a song that was often played on the radio there several years ago. I needed to describe the distinctive quality of the city's midmorning light in

winter, the intense hush at nightfall, the earnestness
with which the trolley conductors inspected tickets, the
idiosyncratic design of the children's schoolbags, a leaning tower in the financial district, a street in which every
shop sold parakeets, and the Corniche on the fairest of
days. My ears popped again and I thought I heard hers
pop too. She firmly took my arm when we reached the
lobby. She pushed me through the revolving door into
the plaza in front of the building.

The airport shuttle was waiting at the curb. Pulling
open the door for me, she murmured, "Stay safe,
Donovan. Enjoy the flight."

The driver looked very familiar.

Adachi Pimentel

KEN KALFUS is the author of three previous novels, including a National Book Award finalist, *A Disorder Peculiar to the Country*. One of his three collections of short stories, *Pu-239 and Other Russian Fantasies*, was a finalist for the PEN/Faulkner Award and the basis for the HBO film *Pu-239*. His books have been translated into more than ten foreign languages. He lives in Philadelphia.

milkweed
EDITIONS

Founded as a nonprofit organization in 1980, Milkweed
Editions is an independent publisher. Our mission is to
identify, nurture, and publish transformative literature,
and build an engaged community around it.

Milkweed Editions is based in Bdé Óta Othuŋwe
(Minneapolis) within Mní Sota Makhoče, the
traditional homeland of the Dakhóta people. Residing
here since time immemorial, Dakhóta people still
call Mní Sota Makhoče home, with four federally
recognized Dakhóta nations and many more Dakhóta
people residing in what is now the state of Minnesota.
Due to continued legacies of colonization, genocide,
and forced removal, generations of Dakhóta people
remain disenfranchised from their traditional
homeland. Presently, Mní Sota Makhoče has become
a refuge and home for many Indigenous nations and
peoples, including seven federally recognized
Ojibwe nations. We humbly encourage our readers
to reflect upon the historical legacies held
in the lands they occupy.

milkweed.org

Milkweed Editions, an independent nonprofit publisher, gratefully acknowledges sustaining support from our Board of Directors; the Alan B. Slifka Foundation and its president, Riva Ariella Ritvo-Slifka; the Amazon Literary Partnership; the Ballard Spahr Foundation; *Copper Nickel*; the McKnight Foundation; the National Endowment for the Arts; the National Poetry Series; the Target Foundation; and other generous contributions from foundations, corporations, and individuals. Also, this activity is made possible by the voters of Minnesota through a Minnesota State Arts Board Operating Support grant, thanks to a legislative appropriation from the arts and cultural heritage fund. For a full listing of Milkweed Editions supporters, please visit milkweed.org.

The author is grateful for the generous support of La Maison Dora Maar and the Nancy B. Negley Artists Residency Program.

Interior design and typesetting
by Mary Austin Speaker

Bulmer was created in the late 1780s or early 1790s.
This late "transitional" typeface was designed
by William Martin for William Bulmer,
who ran the Shakespeare Press.